Oxbow Island Gang

Lobster Graveyard

by Rae Chalmers

illustrated by Jamie Hogan

For Sean.
Wishing you many
happy outdoor adventures
with family and friends.
Rae Chalmers

Oxbow Island Gang: Lobster Graveyard
Copyright © 2021 Rae Chalmers

ISBN: 978-1-63381-250-5

Illustrated by Jamie Hogan

Designed and produced by:
Maine Authors Publishing
12 High Street, Thomaston, Maine
www.maineauthorspublishing.com

Printed in the United States of America

For Barrett and Mika

N

W   E

S

Gulf of Maine

Atlantic Ave

Hidden Pond

Maple Str

Seabreeze B&

gift shop

Wharf St

W

Mooney's

Ferry Landin

Beaver Pond

Shore Bird Restaurant

Eagle Pond

gas

Tennis CLUB

Birch grove

CLUB Road

Yacht CLUB

1

Berend Houtman's mother drove into the ferry terminal parking lot. Bear, as Berend was called, opened his door before the car stopped moving. His head swiveled side to side as he searched for Olivia. She was always running. She'd probably appear at his side before his feet touched the ground. They had only a week to get ready for the best Halloween ever. They couldn't start building anything or making costumes before they got to Oxbow Island, but they could plan. Strategy was going to be key to executing an epic Halloween that would get them into *The Guinness Book of World Records*. Intent on succeeding, Bear had managed to persuade his parents and teachers in Hopkinton, Massachusetts, to let him do an ocean research project on Oxbow Island instead of going to school. Convincing them to let him skip school had to be harder than building the biggest pumpkin pyramid ever seen on Earth.

Weird that Olivia wasn't there to meet him. In September she had convinced him that Oxbow Island was the best place to be for Halloween. There was a haunted house at the Grange Hall and a pumpkin pie eating contest at the American Legion. With all the artists on the island, the costumes tended toward the homemade and crazy: dancing robots that lit up, groups of children encased in a sinking ship, pretending to be the Titanic, and flocks of dogs wearing chicken costumes. Kids from Portland took the ferry out to Oxbow to go trick-or-treating, doubling the small island's population for one evening.

Bear looked around again as his mother placed his suitcase beside him.

"I thought Olivia was meeting you."

"Me too."

"Want me to wait?"

Bear said, "No," but his mother remained beside him. Relieved, he leaned into her.

"There she is!" Julia Houtman said. She rushed to greet Olivia.

Bear had never seen Olivia move so slowly. She looked at her feet and didn't even notice Mrs. Houtman until she was swept into a hug. In September, Bear had seen Olivia angry, scared, exhausted, worried, even happy. But whatever she was feeling now was a mystery to him as she shuffled toward Bear without making eye contact. Had she changed her mind about Halloween? It had been her idea for him to visit and his idea to build the biggest pumpkin pyramid ever. He hadn't told her that part yet. Now he wasn't sure she would like the idea at all.

"I'm going to get back on the road," Julia Houtman said, hugging Bear and whispering, "I love you."

Before stepping into the car, she looked at her son and said, "Bear, don't leave your schoolwork to the end. We're trusting you to do what you committed to." Her stern look wasn't very convincing. "When Olivia's at school, you do your schoolwork, and when she's home you two can work on Halloween. Deal?" She didn't wait for an answer. "Now you two try to stay out of trouble. Leave the detective work to the police. Okay?"

Their heads nodded in agreement, but Bear rolled his eyes and mumbled to Olivia, "What's her problem? It's just Halloween. What does she think we're going to do?" They both waved as Bear's mother beeped the car's horn and drove away.

The mumbled unintelligible announcement for the Oxbow Island Ferry blasted out over the loudspeaker.

"We gotta go!" Bear picked up his suitcase and started running for the boat before he realized Olivia was plodding behind him. He stopped to wait and raised a hand to silently ask, *What's wrong?*

"One small problem with your mother's plan," Olivia said. "I'm not going back to that school. Ever."

"I thought you liked it."

After being homeschooled for most of her life, Olivia had decided to return to public school one week into the seventh grade. She had stopped attending school in the first grade when her father had a tragic accident that left him in a wheelchair. Six years after the accident, the last time Bear was on Oxbow Island, she had realized that her dad didn't need her help at home anymore.

"You're on the cross-country team. Gramma says you're their best runner. You even beat the boys." That was no surprise to Bear, who knew that running was Olivia's favorite form of transportation.

"Yeah, that's the problem." Olivia dragged her hand on the railing as they walked down the ramp to the car ferry. She flashed her school pass at Hector, the deckhand. His square jaw broke into an easy smile, flashing broad, white teeth.

"Hey, Buddy." Hector spotted Bear. "Don't tell me you got kicked out of school again."

Bear felt his face flush. "No. We're getting ready for Halloween." He had assumed he would be greeted as a returning hero, not someone who got kicked out of school in

4

the first week of sixth grade, as he had been when he visited the island in September. He had imagined the residents of Oxbow Island would remember him for cracking an environmental crime, catching a dangerous poacher, and putting his life on the line for wildlife. Bear's head drooped to match Olivia's.

"You!" The athletic young deckhand turned his attention to Olivia. "Thought you had a meet today."

"Canceled," she said.

"Really?" Hector looked confused. "You know, the whole island's coming to watch you run next Friday. You better make us proud." He raised his calloused brown hand in the air for a high five, but Olivia turned away.

"Perfect," she mumbled, punching the cabin door as she walked past.

When Bear caught up with her, she was rubbing the red knuckles on her right hand. "Leave your suitcase by the wheelchair." Olivia nodded toward the chair that rode back and forth on the ferry. Children fought over who got to sit in it and the elderly hoped they never needed it. She glanced at the other islanders: reading, visiting, and potentially eavesdropping. "We'll go to the top deck," she said, heading up the stairs without waiting for Bear.

He found her on the third deck leaning out over the railing with the hint of a smile on her face.

"Look." She pointed at three seals following a fishing boat into the bait pier. They grinned as they watched the seals rolling in the cold water of Casco Bay.

"Look! There's a loon."

"Seems early for them to be in the ocean," Olivia said.

The friends relaxed and settled into their habit of wildlife spotting. The sights, sounds, and smells of coastal Maine had a magnetic pull on Bear and Olivia's hearts, tugging them toward home.

The captain sounded the boat's horn, they covered their ears, and the ferry glided into the harbor. Bear felt himself relaxing as the salty fragrance of the Atlantic Ocean floated over him. They sat on the bench, enjoying the comfortable silence of friends who don't need to prove anything to each other. Bear had wanted to start planning their record-setting gigantically huge pumpkin pyramid, but he was distracted by an oil tanker riding low in the water, being guided into the harbor by two tugboats. The ferry rocked gently as they crossed another boat's wake.

"I better tell you this while nobody's here." Olivia's voice was low as she glanced behind them. It was the end of October. The day-trippers, summer renters, and leaf-peepers were long gone. They were the only ones riding outside on the top deck. "I don't know what to do. The cross-country coach is a jerk. That's why I didn't run today. The meet wasn't canceled."

She had Bear's undivided attention. Olivia never called anybody names, and when Bear did, she usually corrected him, just like his grandmother. Things must be bad for her to call a grown-up a *jerk* and skip a meet.

"He doesn't pay any attention to the girls. Not that they care. I don't know why they're even on the team. The coach takes off running with the boys and the girls walk around talking. Except for Ubah, most of them seem like they don't like running."

"Ubah? What kind of name is Ubah?"

Olivia looked at him like he was an idiot. "Her parents are from Somalia, and I really like her," she snapped.

"Okay. Sorry. Geez."

"I'd never heard the name before either," Olivia said in an almost-apology. She looked up from her swollen red knuckles and grinned at Bear. "And I didn't know where Somalia was. Basically, I like her because she lets me sit with her and her friends at lunch."

"Nothing wrong with that." Bear had his own experiences of not having anyone to sit with in the lunchroom. It wasn't a bad way to figure out who your friends were.

"School's hard. Not the work, but the kid stuff. It's bad enough being from the island." Olivia wiggled her fingers as she examined her bruised hand. "The other kids make fun of us. We don't dress like them or act like them. You know?"

Bear nodded. Oxbow Island's small school went only through the fifth grade and had fewer than forty students. From the sixth grade through high school, the island children took the ferry every day to attend school in Portland. It was a big adjustment to be at a new school surrounded by hundreds of children and unfamiliar teachers.

"The other kids in my grade from the island had last year to figure things out. I'm the only one who's new as a seventh-grader." She looked at Bear. "And I'm the only island girl in the whole seventh grade." She looked down, rubbed her swollen knuckles, and spoke so quietly, Bear had to lean toward her. "I thought I was missing something. All those years at home with Dad." Olivia gazed toward Porcupine Island as the ferry steamed past.

From the distance of the ferry, the island didn't look much bigger than the pitcher's mound at Fenway Park. It was crowded with pine trees jutting out like the quills on an anxious porcupine. An osprey nest sat atop a platform on a tall pole near the shore. They always checked to see if there was an osprey perched on the edge. Bear and Olivia leaned forward, craning their heads toward the nest site.

"Who's that?" Bear pointed at a small wooden boat with an outboard motor near Porcupine Island.

"Probably some island kid, Lenny or Miguel or Asa. Most of them have a few traps of their own. They make good money. They stay close to shore where it's shallower because they haul the traps up by hand."

Bear sat back in his seat, impressed. He couldn't imagine pulling one of those heavy lobster traps up through the water into a tiny tippy boat. He couldn't imagine being alone in a boat in the Atlantic Ocean. After a pause, Bear remembered Olivia's problems. "You must have made friends on the cross-country team."

"No. After the first meet, the coach made sure I always ran up in front with the guys. Then he'd send me back to run with the other girls. That's how I got to know Ubah. She was never too far behind me. The two of us would run back together to the rest of the girls." Olivia started pulling on her bangs. "It was okay. It was fine. That's what I thought." She turned toward Bear. "I didn't know the coach was using me to make fun of the boys. Because I'm faster than them. He'd yell at them, 'You got girled!'" When Bear didn't say anything, she explained, "That's bad. Being beaten by a girl is supposed to be bad—embarrassing. I don't know." Olivia exhaled loudly and stared toward Oxbow Island.

Bear sat up. He didn't know what to say. "You're always faster than me." He didn't like being slow, but that had nothing to do with Olivia being a girl. Olivia ran every day, all day; it was who she was, how she traveled.

"After a while, the guys were elbowing me and trying to trip me. They did it to Ubah too. That made me run faster to get away from them. But Ubah kept slowing down to stay farther behind them. Neither one of us wanted to be in sight of the guys. We didn't know why they were picking on us until this slow guy—"

"Like me."

"Maybe." Olivia smiled. "He warned me. In a nice way. This slow guy, Ezrah, said he was afraid they were going to hurt me." Olivia shook her head. "They wanted to hurt me for running." She slumped back on the red bench.

Bear's eyes widened. Olivia was the toughest person he knew, and she seemed scared.

"Today, I went to the coach and told him. He thought it was funny. Said he was glad to see they were competitive, tough. He asked me if I wanted to hang out with the girls or run faster. And the way he said *girls*, it sounded like he was swearing. No wonder they don't try." Olivia looked down. "I'm not going back to school."

"You can outrun them."

She nodded.

"And even Mr. Mooney says you have a mean right cross." Bear brought up the owner of Mooney's Market as a joke, but Olivia didn't smile.

"I'd rather stay home than get kicked out of school for fighting," she said quietly. "Today, in the cafeteria, they threw food at us."

"What?"

"It's worse."

Bear didn't know what could be worse than that.

"I sit with Ubah and her friends. They're all Somali-Americans. Some people call them refugee girls. They dress differently and they get teased and bullied for that. I'm just attracting more attention to them. I can't do that. But I don't have anywhere else to go. And," she gestured toward Hector on the lower deck, "people are planning on coming to next Friday's meet to see me run. It's the last meet."

"The State Championship?"

"We won't qualify for that. The girl's team is terrible. The other girls all stick together, like a pack. A back-of-the-pack pack. They don't even try. I can't blame them, really."

"What about Tuba?" Bear smiled at his joke.

"That's not funny." Olivia scowled at him. "Her name's Ubah." "She never runs at the meets. I asked her why and she said she's not strong enough, but that doesn't make sense. Dad says to be a refugee you have to be strong. You have to be a survivor. I know she's fast."

As Bear and Olivia considered her tangled problems, the prow of the ferry squared up with the island's dock. They were almost there. Problems always seemed smaller when they were on Oxbow Island.

"It's Friday," Bear said. "We have the weekend. We'll think of something."

"Maybe." Olivia did not sound reassured. She pointed. "There's your grandmother. The Professor's with her too." Olivia jumped up and ran to the stairs.

"Hey! We didn't talk about Halloween," Bear hollered at her back.

2

"Buckaroo Bear!" his grandmother hollered as she waved her hands high above her head.

"Mr. Bear," the Professor called out. The exceptionally tall black man made his best attempt to bow while balancing on crutches.

"You're out of the wheelchair!" Bear said. Seven weeks earlier, the Professor had been injured when they attempted to catch a poacher on Oxbow Island's wooded trails.

"I still use it when Victor wants to race."

Olivia almost smiled at the Professor's mention of her father racing him in a wheelchair. With six years of experience, no one was faster or could do more tricks in a wheelchair than Victor Anaya.

Bear closed his eyes and breathed in the salty moist air. It was good to be back on Oxbow Island. His silent appreciation was cut short. A furry force slammed into his chest and knocked him backward. His eyes jerked open and he was face-to-snout with Honey the Wonder Dog, his grandmother's golden retriever, the dog's front paws firmly planted on his chest. "Want to dance?" Bear placed his hands on the dog's paws and stepped from side to side. Honey followed his lead. "No leash?" Bear asked his grandmother.

Honey dropped her front paws back to the ground and appeared offended by the question.

"Well, we don't have an animal control officer anymore." Sally Parker mussed Bear's unruly brown curls. "What happened to my short, round grandson?" she asked, putting her hands on his shoulders.

"Hey!" It was good to be back on Oxbow Island until his grandmother embarrassed him.

"Olivia," his grandmother continued, "I think Bear's starting to look like a runner—"

"Gramma!" Bear cut her off. He narrowed his round green eyes, pulled his lips over his teeth, and shook his head *no*.

Sally Parker matched his expression, feature for feature, with a few wrinkles, prompting Olivia and the Professor to grin. "What I meant, Buckaroo, is that you look fantastic, taller and very fit." She opened her arms.

Bear hugged her so hard he lifted her feet off the ground.

"Another year and I'll be as tall as you." He looked around. Most of the leaves were off the trees. The Goofy Gull Gift Shop had closed for the season. No kids rushed to jump off the dock into the frigid Atlantic Ocean. There wasn't a crowd pushing to board the ferry and return to Portland. "It's so peaceful." Bear turned to Olivia. "Nothing like all the craziness the last time I was here."

"Half of that was you," Olivia said.

"Me?"

The Professor and Sally Parker nodded.

"We mean that in the best possible way," his grandmother said as she draped an arm over his shoulder and they began the steep walk up Wharf Street.

They were all going to the home of Viola Frost, Sally Parker's ninety-year-old neighbor, for a potluck supper. After the Professor's accident, his friends had added a wheelchair ramp to the front of Mrs. Frost's house and he had stayed with her ever since. On any given day it was a toss-up as to who was helping whom. His own house was on the opposite side of Maple Street. The wheelchair ramp meant that Victor Anaya could roll right in and visit both of his friends. Mrs. Frost was grateful for the company afforded by the ramp but swore she would be dead and buried before anyone would see her in a wheelchair. Of course, she never said that in front of Victor.

"Olivia and Berend, what are your Halloween plans?" Mrs. Frost asked as she brought her three-bean casserole to the table.

"I don't know," Olivia said. It seemed that her gloom from the boat ride had found her again.

"I do." Finally, the moment Bear had been waiting for. He put his elbows on the table and leaned forward. "We're going to be in *The Guinness Book of Records*."

"We are?" Olivia scrunched her brown eyes close together and peered at Bear.

"I heard about a man in Georgia." Victor Anaya tapped his fork on the edge of his plate. "What was his name?" Victor looked at the others seated round the table. "Mike Mills!" He set his fork down with a loud clunk. "Mike Mills tried to get into that *Guinness Book*. He towed a five-thousand-pound SUV behind his wheelchair. Can you imagine?"

Bear shook his head, frustrated by the interruption. "I have it all figured out. We're going to make the world's biggest pumpkin pyramid. Ever."

The Professor looked at Victor. "There's a fellow in Finland. He pulled two cars behind his wheelchair. Apparently, this is an area of intense international competition."

Bear wiggled in his seat and cleared his throat. "Halloween! We were talking about my plan for Halloween—"

The Professor turned his gaze on Bear and cut him off. "You two have demonstrated impressive and stylistic stacking skills." The Professor was referring to the coastal mosaic they had created when they stacked his firewood. "I have not acquired an advanced degree in pumpkin engineering. Still, it occurs to me that the world's largest pumpkin pyramid would require a vast quantity of pumpkins, and we reside on a diminutive island."

"I thought of that." Bear was confident. He had figured out all the details. "Everyone on Oxbow Island has a garden, and everyone on Oxbow Island is generous. Right?"

"We're not hoarders," Mrs. Frost said proudly. "We keep what we need and share the rest."

"Works for everything from automobile repair to zucchini," Bear's grandmother said.

Victor added, "In the summer, John Calvin helps himself to our garden, and in the winter, he shovels us out after every storm."

"Officer Calvin? The island cop?" Bear never would have guessed he was friends with Victor. Island friendships, island relatives—if you didn't keep them straight you could get yourself into trouble in a hurry. There was nothing worse than making fun of some guy's mustache before discovering you're talking to his mother.

His grandmother and her neighbors nodded in agreement.

"I thought his first name was Calvin." Bear speared a green bean with his fork. "But it's really John?"

"We could put up a sign at Mooney's Market," Olivia said.

"Zoe could mention it to people when she's driving the taxi," Viola Frost added.

Bear smiled. He knew they'd like his idea. "We'll get the word out and everyone'll bring pumpkins to Gramma's house. We can start building tomorrow." Bear sat back in his chair.

The Professor leaned forward. "Three-sided or four-sided pyramid?"

Victor followed up. "How tall does it have to be to be the biggest?"

The questions kept coming:

"How wide?"

"Is it hollow or solid?"

"Can we use pie pumpkins?"

"Is it the biggest because it's the tallest? Widest? Or uses the most pumpkins?"

The smile faded from Bear's face. Maybe he hadn't thought of everything.

Mrs. Frost tapped the Professor's arm. "Would you get that sketch pad and pencil from my puzzle table for Berend?" It was clear that even on crutches the Professor moved faster than Mrs. Frost.

He retrieved the pad and handed it to Bear. "Mr. Bear, would you be kind enough to share a sketch?"

Bear slid the sketch pad to Olivia, who shrugged her confusion. She looked around the table and then slid it back to Mrs. Frost and the Professor.

Victor Anaya spoke, filling the silence with his rich, booming voice. "Bear, your first decision is whether you want a three- or four-sided pyramid. A three-sided pyramid will use fewer pumpkins."

Bear nodded. "Sure. Yeah. Sounds good."

"Let's say you have ten pumpkins at the base on each of the three sides." The Professor sketched as he talked. "And each row has one fewer pumpkin than the row beneath it—"

Mrs. Frost interrupted the Professor. "You'll need one hundred sixty-six pumpkins."

"How'd you do that?" Bear and Olivia gasped. Mrs. Frost's body may have slowed down over the previous nine decades, but her brain was the fastest at the table.

The Professor scribbled on his pad, looked up, and said, "I believe you've made a mistake, Viola. By my calculations, it's one sixty-five."

She patted his arm gently. "I added one more on top where the three sides come together. You don't want a flat-topped pyramid, do you?"

Everyone looked at the long-retired teacher and agreed: they did not.

"Two problems," Olivia said. "First, one hundred sixty-five pumpkins, that's a lot of pumpkins. Second, a pyramid with a base of only ten pumpkins on each side doesn't sound like the biggest in the world to me."

"Your points are contradictory but valid," the Professor said. He slid the sketch pad away from his dinner plate. Silence settled over the table as the friends and neighbors stared at their food.

Sally Parker tapped her hands on the table beside her dinner plate. "Let's ask everyone for their spare pumpkins. We'll see how many we get. No matter what, it will be the biggest pumpkin pyramid ever seen on Oxbow Island. Maybe it will be the biggest in Maine, New England, the United States, or the world. We won't know unless we try."

Bear wasn't sure.

"The fun is in the trying," his grandmother said with genuine enthusiasm.

"Everyone can make a poster asking for pumpkins, explaining why we need them," Olivia said. "Pass me the sketch pad."

3

Before the dishes were even dried, the grown-ups released Olivia, Bear, and Honey to post their signs
around the island. The sugar maples on the street cast eerie
shadows beneath the orange glow of the full moon. They
turned onto Wharf Street and the moon became a bea-
con lighting the way. Heading off at a trot, the three loped
downhill toward Water Street, where all the island's busi-
nesses were located.

"Mooney's Market," Olivia hollered over her shoulder as
she turned right onto Water Street.

Bear followed. When it came to running with Olivia,
he always followed. Her training with the boys' cross-country team had increased the gap between them. Honey kept
pace while taking her usual side trips: down to the beach to
roll in the seaweed, then up the steps of the Seabreeze Bed

and Breakfast to get a treat from a man relaxing in a rocking chair. The golden retriever was never far away.

The market was closed for the evening, but they taped a sign to the door. The owner, Mike Mooney, or his deli clerk, Wanda, would post it next to the coffee pot when they opened for business on Saturday morning. At the café, they slid the sign under the door. If Linda didn't post it, she would tell everyone about the pumpkin pyramid as she made their breakfast sandwiches. That was even better.

"Dudes, are you two terrorizing the island again?" A smooth singer's voice teased them.

"Zoe!" Bear ran to the side of the dented, cherry-red taxi and greeted the thirty-year-old driver. "Hugged any trees lately?"

She shook her head. "Missed you too. What are you up to now?"

"We need pumpkins," Bear said as Olivia passed a poster through the passenger window. "Lots of them."

"Can you tell your passengers?" Olivia asked.

Zoe nodded with enthusiasm and her dreadlocks bounced on her shoulders. "Totally." Then the taxi rolled forward. "Gotta meet the nine," she hollered, referring to the next ferry from Portland.

Bear and Olivia trotted toward the fish house, a weather-worn building facing Lobster Cove. The six lobstermen on Oxbow Island used it for storing and repairing their gear. The lights would be on well before five o'clock the next morning and by two o'clock in the afternoon they'd be cleaning up for the day and swapping stories.

"No one'll be there," Olivia said and slowed to a walk at the top of the boat ramp. "They'll see it before they go out in the morning." She stopped and sniffed the air as Bear joined her.

"What?" Bear came to an abrupt stop as Olivia held up her hand in front of him.

Olivia grinned. "Smell that?" There was a warm nutty scent in the crisp fall air. She whispered to Bear, "Hiram Wiley. He smokes a pipe." And then she yelled, "Hey, Hi!" before turning back to Bear. "I love saying that. Hey, Hi," she repeated to herself. "He's hard of hearing from all those years with the boat engine. You have to speak up."

As they rounded the corner of the fish house, Bear saw a familiar figure. The moonlight bounced off the figure's shiny bald head, but the full, neatly trimmed silver beard compensated for the lack of hair on top. Smoking a pipe and crocheting a bait bag, Hiram reclined in a battered chair that looked like it had been rescued from the dump.

"What're you doing here so late?" Olivia asked.

"Evening, Olivia. Million-dollar view." He gestured toward the ocean and Bear noticed that the lobsterman was missing at least one knuckle from each of two fingers on his right hand. Moonlight reflected off the ocean, creating a golden path to the opposite shore. "Shame to miss a full moon on a clear night." He jerked his huge thumb toward Bear and asked, "This Sally Parker's grandson?" Without waiting for an answer, he addressed Bear. "You're keeping fast company, young man. This one," his index finger, the size of a hot dog, jabbed in Olivia's direction, "is going to beat everyone next Friday."

Olivia started shaking her head in protest.

"No need for modesty. My grandson keeps me informed." He looked back at the crochet hook and twine in his lap. "We're mighty proud."

Olivia was silent. Bear sensed that Hiram Wiley was not a man you argued with. His sharp, craggy features would not accept news of Olivia dropping off the cross-country team.

"Mr. Wiley," Bear began.

"What?"

"Mr. Wiley." Bear spoke louder.

"Hi," the lobsterman said.

"Hi," Bear replied. He thought they were past greetings.

"Call him *Hi*," Olivia whispered. "And speak up!"

Bear started over. "We have some posters." He held them in front of the lobsterman's face in case he hadn't heard. "We're asking for pumpkins so we can build a pyramid." Hiram Wiley read in the moonlight. "It's going to be huge. If we can get enough pumpkins." Bear looked at the lobsterman's unexpressive face. It could have been carved from granite. Even the pipe was fixed in place, but his hands never stopped working. He didn't need to see what he was crocheting any more than he needed ten complete fingers. Bear stared at the injured hand. He exhaled and his voice squeaked. "Can we put a poster here?"

Hiram lowered his head once in an abbreviated nod and jerked his thumb toward the shack.

Olivia stapled the poster to the shack before Hiram's hand returned to his crocheting. She tapped Bear on the shoulder and tilted her head toward the road.

"Thanks, Hi," they hollered over their shoulders as they jogged up the boat ramp to Water Street. As they stepped onto the sidewalk, they saw Honey trotting down the street, leading the way home, her silky golden tail waving above her, glowing in the moonlight.

Olivia slowed her pace and ran beside Bear.

"Olivia," Bear began tentatively. She didn't look at him, but she didn't sprint ahead either, so he continued. "What Mr. Wiley—Hi—said about you running, and Hector too, when we got on the boat—" He struggled to find words that wouldn't make her mad and lowered his voice. "They're counting on you. The whole island's counting on you." Her expression and her pace hadn't changed. It was as if he hadn't spoken. In frustration he blurted, "You love running. You have to stay on the cross-country team."

"I love running and that's why I have to quit."

Honey waited patiently for Bear and Olivia as they walked up Sally Parker's porch steps. There was something pale sticking out of both sides of her mouth.

"What've you got?" Bear asked as he knelt in front of the golden retriever. She dropped it in his hand and Bear's mouth fell open. It was a lobster claw, the color of a bleached peach, faded from sun or age. It was nearly as long as his forearm. "Where did you—" he began and then looked at Olivia.

"That's huge. I've never— Maybe we could use it for a Halloween costume."

"The Lobster Monster!" Bear said in a scary voice and raised his arms like a zombie.

"We'd need two, and there's no way we'll find another lobster claw that big."

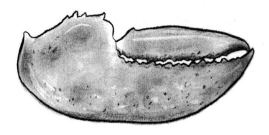

4

"Buckaroo Bear! Get up!" Sally Parker shouted up the stairs Saturday morning. "You have to see this."

Bear and Honey stumbled down the stairs, tripping over each other. "What?" he mumbled as he rubbed his eyes and moved slowly toward the front windows. "Pumpkins!" he shouted. "How many do you think there are?" He didn't wait for an answer. He raced upstairs with Honey on his heels. He had to get dressed and start building. Five minutes later he was on the front porch watching Mike Mooney drive off after depositing more pumpkins in the front yard.

Next door, Mrs. Frost's window opened. He could see her skinny arm and the lumpy knuckles on her hand clenched in a raised fist. He stretched his arm toward her house and made a fist too. "Kaboom," they shouted in unison as they opened their fists and raised their arms. For months that had been their shared gesture of success.

"Berend, I can't see all of them." Her head stuck out the window and a long white braid swung below the windowsill. She wasn't ready for the day until her hair had been unbraided, combed, braided again, and pinned in a circle around her head. She would not leave her house until her hair was *just so*. "How many are there? We need one hundred sixty-six."

"Mr. Bear, it appears you have your work cut out for you." The Professor leaned on his crutches, balancing awkwardly on Mrs. Frost's front porch.

Bear grinned back. "Yup!"

Slowly the Professor hobbled down the ramp. "By my calculations you are a few pumpkins short of a pyramid."

"But look." Bear gestured toward all the round and oblong, ribbed and smooth, large and small pumpkins deposited in his grandmother's front yard. "Let's see." He started counting. "Sixty-two, sixty-three, sixty-four." It was a lot of pumpkins, but not nearly enough. He kicked the pumpkin closest to him.

"Mr. Bear," the Professor said, balancing beside him, "the day is young. More will undoubtedly be delivered."

"You think?"

"All the time." The Professor laid a comforting hand on Bear's shoulder. "Patience is a virtue."

After breakfast, Bear returned to the front yard and found more pumpkins, but he had learned his lesson: a lot of pumpkins might not be enough. He tried to be patient. He could sort them while he waited for more to arrive. He needed thirty large ones for the base and then twenty-seven that were a little smaller. Each row would have to have pumpkins of the same height or everything would collapse. Stacking firewood had taught him a few things. He focused on sorting the pumpkins by size.

Bear smelled earthy pipe smoke before he heard Hiram Wiley.

"Corker of a day!"

"You're not on your boat?"

"My boy Fuzzy's hauling traps today. My grandson's friend, Miguel, he's the sternman on Saturdays, when he doesn't have a game. He's about your age. You know him?"

Bear didn't know Miguel. He didn't know most of the year-round kids on Oxbow Island. He had met Olivia in September, when she'd helped him track down the person who was trying to rid the island of beavers. He shook his head. Hiram Wiley appeared to have used up all his words for the day, so Bear filled the silence. "I'm sorting the pumpkins by size, but we don't have enough. I'm hoping more will show up. The Professor says patience is a virtue. I'm not really virtuous." Now Bear had run out of words.

"You get the chicken by hatching the egg. Not by smashing it." Hiram Wiley struck a match and raised it to his pipe.

"Morning," Olivia called out as she turned the corner onto Maple Street.

Bear shook his head with relief: relief that he didn't have to make sense of pumpkins, eggs, and chickens. And relief that he didn't have to talk to this stone-faced man for another minute. "Olivia! Look!"

"Yeah." She gestured toward the pumpkins. "Not a bad start." Turning to Hiram, she grinned and said, "Hey, Hi."

Hiram dipped his head in acknowledgment. "Came to see what you need." With one giant hand he scooped up the biggest pumpkin in the yard. "I was thinking rebar, metal."

Bear couldn't stop staring at the two stubby fingers on his right hand, each missing a knuckle or two.

"Lost them when I was thirteen." Had he read Bear's mind? "Working as a sternman on my pop's boat. Hand caught in the winch." He set the pumpkin down gently beside his rubber work boots. "I was lucky that day."

It hardly sounded lucky to Bear. He looked at Olivia. She knew more about good luck and bad accidents than he ever wanted to know, and she nodded her agreement.

"You think we need rebar?" she asked.

"Three-sided?" Hiram arranged the nine largest pumpkins in a triangle on the grass between them.

Olivia nodded.

"Hollow?" He carefully balanced a smaller triangle of six pumpkins on top of the base.

Olivia nodded.

"Want it to stand for more than ten minutes?" He placed three pumpkins on top of the six.

"Yes!" Both Olivia and Bear answered as Hiram set the final pumpkins on the pyramid.

From behind them they heard shuffling, followed by, "Excuse me, please."

As Hiram, Bear, and Olivia turned toward the voice, the pumpkins shifted, slipped, and fell to the ground.

"Ubah!" Olivia said and jogged to meet her friend.

Ubah wore a long-sleeve shirt that came to her knees and matching pants. A lightweight scarf was wrapped around her head, concealing most of her shiny black hair. Behind her stood a man. His khaki pants and dress shirt were freshly ironed with crisp creases, more appropriate for work in a city office than standing in the middle of an island dirt road.

"Excuse me. I am Amiin Daahir, Ubah's father." He earnestly approached each of them and shook their hands, saying their names and repeating his with a solemn and respectful face. By contrast, his daughter was grinning, giggling, and whispering to Olivia.

Bear watched Olivia with surprise. She had friends he didn't know, friends who giggled and shared secrets he knew nothing about. It was surprising to see a different side to a friend he thought he knew so well.

"Welcome to our humble island. I am delighted to make your acquaintance. My name is Malcolm Yeats."

Bear was startled from his thoughts by the sound of the Professor introducing himself to Ubah's father. Mrs. Frost and Sally Parker joined them. The sight of strangers in the yard was too intriguing to ignore and had drawn them from their homes. This started another round of introductions followed by a brief silence.

"Excuse us, please," Mr. Daahir began. "We've come to your island today to ask for your help." Ubah stepped quietly to her father's side and looked down. "My Ubah wants to run. This is not something girls do in Somalia, but I believe we came here for opportunity and this is what she wants."

The residents of Oxbow Island stood in a semicircle in front of Ubah and her father, listening intently.

"As a father I can compromise for my daughter, but she must respect our values."

Ubah's head dipped so low it was impossible to see her expression. Bear looked at everyone else, trying to guess what values could be revealed in running besides good sportsmanship.

"She must wear the hijab," Mr. Daahir said, and all of the adults nodded as if they knew what he was talking about.

"What's a hijab?" Bear blurted.

Olivia gestured that it was Ubah's head covering.

"For the sake of modesty my daughter must be covered." Mr. Daahir clasped his hands and looked down. "I did not know this was a problem. Yesterday, I went to watch her compete and she was not there."

Bear wondered if Olivia knew she wasn't the only girl to skip the cross-country meet.

"I didn't want to worry you." Ubah spoke softly and touched his sleeve.

"There was a meet yesterday?" Sally Parker looked at Olivia before exchanging glances with the Professor and Mrs. Frost.

Bear had to jump in before any of them could ask Olivia why she hadn't gone to the meet, why she had said it was canceled. "Can't she run with a scarf on her head? What's the big deal?"

Mr. Daahir lifted his hands with the palms facing the sky and shook his head.

Ubah spoke, never lifting her gaze from the pumpkins at her feet. "Coach says,"—they all leaned forward to hear her quiet voice—"I have to wear the proper team uniform." She shook her head. "No head coverings are permitted."

Olivia could run and didn't want to. Ubah wanted to run and couldn't. He could solve one of those problems. "I've got an idea," Bear blurted. "It's Halloween next weekend. Just tell your coach that you're wearing a costume." Bear grinned at his brilliant solution and looked at the faces around him. He was surprised by their expressions.

"Mr. Bear..." "Berend..." "Buckaroo..." "Bear..." With varying degrees of shock, reprimand, and offense, they spoke over each other and then there was silence.

"What? What? I'm just saying—"

Mr. Daahir took a small step forward, and Bear took a step backward as he looked into the man's eyes.

Ubah's father took a breath and spoke slowly, choosing his words. "This is not a costume. My daughter is not requesting candy. This is our culture, our customs, our beliefs."

"Ubah, dear." Mrs. Frost gently tapped her cane on the grass in front of her. "Did the coach specifically say, 'No head coverings'?"

Ubah nodded without looking up.

"We're expecting a cold spell at the end of the week. Wonder what the coach would say if most of the team wore knit hats? Strictly for warmth, of course. He couldn't object to your head scarf and let them wear hats. Parents would be understandably upset if he sent the team out underdressed."

"Why would they do that for me?"

"We don't need all of them—" Olivia began.

"You won't know unless you ask," Sally Parker said. "Olivia, if we buy several dozen matching knit hats, can you help Ubah ask the other boys and girls to wear them?"

Bear looked at Olivia. Nobody else knew she wanted to quit the team. Her head turned to the side as Ubah reached for her friend's fingers.

"Will you help me? Everyone respects you. If you ask, they'll do it." Ubah's voice was little more than a whisper.

Olivia finally responded as the cherry-red taxi screeched to a stop in front of Sally Parker's house, but only Bear heard his friend mumble, "They don't respect me." He stayed by her side and tried to read her expression. The pride of Oxbow Island wasn't the only reason it was important for Olivia to remain on the cross-country team.

As the others gathered around the bright, dented minivan and greeted Zoe and her passenger Victor Anaya, Olivia and Bear huddled together.

"What're you going to do?"

"What can I do? They want my help, but they don't know—" With each word her voice became quieter. "Everything was better before." She looked at Bear. "When running was fun."

"Mr. Bear," the Professor called out, "what's seventy-four plus seventeen?"

Bear looked toward the taxi and saw that they were unloading more pumpkins. He began to smile before catching sight of Olivia's gloomy expression. "Not enough," he answered, and turned back to Olivia. "We'll think of something. We always do."

Victor rolled over in his wheelchair and looked concerned. "Everything okay? We thought you'd be excited about the pumpkins."

Bear watched Olivia's face shift as a forced smile lifted the outer corners of her mouth. "Yeah, Dad. It's great. Just planning. You know."

Victor looked skeptical as Hiram Wiley and Amiin Daahir joined them.

"Heading to the fish house," Hiram said to Victor. "You coming?"

Victor looked at Olivia again.

"I'm fine, Dad. Really. Go."

Bear was curious about the unlikely threesome. "What're you doing?"

Mr. Daahir's grin stretched from ear to ear. "I am a taxi-driving engineer. Mr. Wiley has tools and an idea, and I'm told Mr. Anaya can build anything. Together we will construct the framework for your record-breaking pumpkin pyramid." He bent at the waist in a slight bow toward Olivia and Bear. "That is the least I can do for my daughter's friends."

When the three men left, Bear and Olivia looked at each other. Olivia raised her hands in defeat. Her mouth hung open. She was speechless.

"What's a taxi-driving engineer?" Bear asked.

"My father was an engineer in Somalia," Ubah said quietly behind him. "Here, he drives a taxi."

Bear spun around, embarrassed again. "Sorry," he mumbled, "about the Halloween costume thing."

Ubah nodded politely.

"Kids," Sally Parker said, the Professor beside her, "we're going off on the next ferry. We have to buy those hats for the team. Mrs. Frost will be here if you need anything. You can't really work on the pyramid until they've finished the framework, so why don't you two show Ubah the island?"

As his grandmother and the Professor climbed into the taxi, Bear watched Olivia and Ubah trot down the dirt road, leaving him behind. Their strides synchronized as their heads leaned toward each other in conversation. Alone, Bear turned toward the porch.

Mrs. Frost had been there all along with both hands resting on her cane. Her soft blue eyes looked into his and asked, *What's wrong, Berend?* Honey was sleeping at her feet. The dog rose, walked over to Bear, and leaned against his legs. Bear dropped to his knees, wrapped his arms around Honey, and buried his face in the golden retriever's neck.

"Olivia is your friend. Never question that."

Bear looked up at the old woman, who had always been able to read his mind. He shrugged and stoked Honey's silky ears.

Mrs. Frost's face lit up with a smile.

"Bear, come on!" Olivia hollered from the road. They'd come back for him. "Bring Honey too. I want to show Ubah where we jump off the dock."

Honey's tail thumped against his leg. There was no doubt that she wanted to go. Bear took a step toward the road before stopping and turning back to Mrs. Frost. She couldn't run down the road with them. He looked at the tiny woman leaning on her wooden cane and searched for words.

With one firm nod of her head she told him to go. Mrs. Frost wore the warm expression that always accompanied the words: *You're a good boy, Berend.* She called to him, "I hear my puzzle calling. I can't be standing around chitter-chatting all day."

5

Bear was afraid Ubah and Olivia would be too fast for him, but the three ran together, side-by-side, with Honey greeting neighbors, exploring, and rejoining them as she pleased. The air was pleasantly warm as they jogged down Wharf Street toward the water.

"Let's play Runner Says," Olivia said.

Bear and Ubah looked at her blankly.

"We take turns. I'll go first. Runner says, run sideways." She began moving across the road. Ubah and Bear followed her example. At the edge of the road, she tapped Ubah on the back. "You're next."

"Runner says…" Her voice was as quiet as someone in a library. "Runner says…lift your knees as high as you can."

All three children raised their knees above their waists with each step. Bear was relieved when Olivia said, "Your turn, Bear."

High knees had been exhausting, so Bear decided to go for the opposite. "Runner says kick yourself in the butt." He did his best to lift his heels high behind him but discovered this was as challenging as running with his knees pulled up in front. Ubah had no problem. The heels of her worn-down running shoes slapped against the hem of her long shirt. Olivia, in her heavy rubber boots, struggled as much as Bear.

When they got to the intersection of Wharf and Water streets, a gust of wind from the water shook the tall oak tree and pinned a falling leaf against Olivia's forehead. She grinned and waved the leaf above her head. "Runner says, catch a leaf!" she hollered.

Bear and Ubah raced toward the giant oak tree in front of the Seabreeze Bed and Breakfast. Leaves swirled around them as they lurched to the left and then to the right. The leaves rode the breeze, twisting and turning, always out of reach.

Olivia could be heard alternately laughing and cheering from behind them.

Bear fixed his eyes on a leaf sailing toward him and dove forward just as Ubah leapt in front of him, pursuing her own leaf prize. Bear avoided colliding with her, tripped, and fell with a thud onto the bed and breakfast's walkway.

Both forearms and elbows scraped across the brick as his chin bounced off the hard surface. The breath was knocked out of him and he lay on the bricks, stunned. Honey gently nuzzled his face and he rolled onto his back and groaned.

Standing above him staring at his face were Honey, Olivia, Ubah, and a woman who anyone would think was Mrs. Claus were it any closer to Christmas. Her round jolly face, rosy plump cheeks, and twinkly eyes were circled by wisps of glowing white hair.

"Oh, dear. Oh, dear. You poor boy. Don't move. Stay right there." She bustled off.

Bear sat up and Honey lay her head on his shoulder. "I think I'm okay." He inventoried his injuries. The palms of his hands were scraped and dirty. One elbow was bloody. Both ached.

"Your chin is bleeding too," Olivia said, pointing. "I don't think you'll need stitches. Unless"—she paused and made a dramatic face—"you want to go to the hospital on the fireboat."

"No!" Bear made a move to stand.

"No, no, no. Sit right there." The Mrs. Claus look-alike was back with a first aid kit. "Let me get this all cleaned up and then we'll know if we should call the ambulance."

"No!" Bear said as Olivia laughed. The woman meant well, but he was not riding in an ambulance or taking the fireboat to Portland.

"No need to be afraid," she said.

Bear looked at Olivia and Ubah for support, but they were both trying to hide their smiles. "I'm not afraid," he protested and sat back on the ground. It was obvious he wasn't going anywhere until he let this woman use every tool in her first aid kit.

"First, we need a butterfly bandage for that gash on your chin."

"Are you a nurse?" Olivia asked politely.

"Oh, no, dear. I'm a lobster picker. Used to pick crabs but there isn't much money in that anymore. And I clean rooms here." She gestured toward the Bed and Breakfast.

Bear thought he smelled seafood on her hands as she applied a bit of antibiotic cream to his chin.

"Name's Alberta Goodhue," she said with a sing-song voice that rose and fell sweetly as she began to clean the scrape on Bear's elbow. "Your names?"

They politely introduced themselves.

"Well, Bear, Ubah, and Olivia, would you like some cookies? It's not often company lands in my front yard." She laughed at her own joke and wiped her hands on the floral apron tied to her waist, so small it appeared to be child-sized. Without waiting for an answer, she bustled up the steps to the bed and breakfast.

"What does she mean, she picks lobsters? Don't the lobstermen pick them? They take them out of the traps," Bear said.

Ubah nodded her head in agreement, but Olivia looked like she thought he was crazy.

"The meat. She picks out the lobster meat from the shell."

"No," Bear said. "We do that when we eat them. We pick out the meat ourselves, at the table."

"If they get a lobster that's thrown a claw," Alberta Goodhue said as she returned with a plate of cookies.

"They throw their claws?" Bear and Ubah said. This was shocking news.

Olivia knocked them both on the shoulder. "It's just an expression. Means they're missing a claw."

"Oh." Bear was disappointed.

"Or something else is wrong and it can't be sold as a whole lobster, then I pick the meat and they sell that. Get more per pound that way." Alberta sat back on the bottom porch step and munched loudly on a cookie. "They used to take them home or give them away, but then the boys figured they were throwing away good money and they hired me." She reached for another cookie. "I just clean here for the free room and board." She waved a third cookie in the direction of the bed and breakfast behind her.

Alberta Goodhue looked at Ubah. "That's a peculiar get-up you're wearing." She took a bite of her cookie. "Where are you from?"

Ubah's voice was even quieter than usual. "Portland."

"No. Where are you really from—"

A man at the top of the stairs interrupted her. "Good afternoon."

Alberta jumped up at the sound of his voice. "Did you need something, Frank?" She didn't wait for an answer. "This one," she gestured at Bear, "fell and got pretty banged up, so I bandaged him and took some cookies from the kitchen. Hope that's okay."

"Of course, Alberta." Frank Peabody, the owner of the Seabreeze, glided down the steps with a treat for Honey in his hand. "Bear and Olivia, I can't remember the last time I saw you two sit in one place for so long. Who's your friend?"

"This is Ubah. She's on the cross-country team with me."

Ubah dipped her head politely.

"I'm sure you know the whole island will be at the track meet next Friday." Frank scratched Honey's head as she licked up the remaining crumbs from her treat. As he turned to leave, he said to Olivia, "Make us proud." At the top of the stairs he stopped and pivoted in place. "Alberta, remember we have three check-ins today." And then he was gone.

Alberta leaned forward and lowered her voice. "He's a task master. Wants everything just so." She looked intently at each child. "There's no pleasing his kind."

Bear had to agree. Frank did seem fussy: *particular,* as his grandmother would say, or *persnickety,* as Mrs. Frost would say. Of course, both of them were particular and persnickety too.

Olivia's tone suggested she disagreed. "Frank?" She shook her head. "No." She looked at Bear. "We should get going. Can you run?"

"I think so." He lifted each knee slowly before turning to Alberta Goodhue. "Thank you for the Band-Aids and cleaning me up."

He jumped up and sprinted down Water Street toward the fish house, trying to catch Ubah and Olivia.

"Let's see what they're doing with the rebar," Olivia hollered over her shoulder.

All three sped up. "Do you see Honey?" Bear gasped.

They all looked around as they ran.

"She's never too far away," Olivia said.

Ubah's arm shot up as she pointed toward the back of the fish house. The golden retriever sat waiting, her tail swishing back and forth in the sand as she pretended to be an obedient dog.

"What's she got?" Ubah asked as the three of them stopped running and saw the long, stiff coral-colored object coming out of both sides of her mouth.

"Another one!" Bear dropped to his knees in front of the dog. He waved the giant lobster claw above his head. "We have two. We can use it for a Monster Lobster costume." He grinned.

"Give me that!" It was Hiram Wiley. He grabbed the lobster claw from Bear's upstretched hand and hurled it into a clump of beach grass beside them. His voice was hushed and stern as he looked into the faces of each child. "Never tell anyone about that. Never. Do you hear me?" He looked at each of them and waited for them to nod. "You don't know the trouble you'll be in if anyone ever finds out you had that. Do you understand?" He made eye contact with each of them again. Even Honey was frozen in place by his forceful gaze.

"Hey, you're all here." No one had noticed Victor approaching. What had he heard? He seemed happy to see them, not upset about Hiram Wiley's threat. "Come see what we've done." The three children, the golden retriever, and the lobsterman followed Victor Anaya around the weather-beaten shack.

Inside, Amiin Daahir was standing beside a metal pyramid that was taller than he was and looking closely at a piece of paper.

"Wow!" the three children exclaimed. "It's huge."

"Come in. Come in. Please," Mr. Daahir said, and he set down the paper and a pencil on the cluttered workbench beside him.

"It's not done yet," Victor said. "It will need a lot of reinforcement."

"We are assuming that the average pumpkin weighs twelve pounds, and with one hundred and sixty-six pumpkins our calculations predict an approximate mass of," he looked down at his paper, "nineteen hundred ninety-two pounds."

Bear whispered to Olivia, "Mrs. Frost could've done that in her head."

The children surrounded the rebar pyramid.

"It'll be even bigger with a layer of pumpkins stacked against it!" Bear exclaimed. His excitement was cut short by a shuffling sound behind him. Bear turned. He was startled by the sight of a figure slowly moving toward him, dressed in black with a plastic face shield over goggles. Monstrously large leather gloves clutched an outstretched canister.

Bear scurried behind Victor's wheelchair and crouched low to the ground.

"Dad, can we stay and watch Hi weld?" Olivia asked.

Bear felt a flush rise through his face. It was Hiram Wiley. Bear peeked over Victor's shoulder. Hiram was preparing to weld. "Great Halloween costume," Bear tried to joke. Embarrassment and relief flowed through his body as he stood.

"We must be leaving," Mr. Daahir said as he placed a hand on Ubah's shoulder. "You understand the plans?" he asked Hiram, who responded with a nod. "It has been a pleasure to meet all of you," Mr. Daahir added as they stepped out of the fish house.

"It's not safe to watch," Victor said to Olivia, "unless you're dressed like Hi. Time to head home."

Bear was left alone with Hiram, who could have been a character in a horror movie. "I think I'll go help Mrs. Frost. With that puzzle. She's got a puz…" Bear mumbled. He stepped outside and whispered, "Come on Honey." He looked down at the golden retriever and hoped with all his might that her mouth was empty. She cocked her head and looked at him with her sweetest face. "Let's go home before you get us in any more trouble," Bear whispered in her ear.

They were almost at the bed and breakfast when Bear dashed back toward the fish house. He looked around him. No one was in sight. He darted into the tall grass and easily found the lobster claw that had been taken from him. Based on Hiram Wiley's response, Bear knew it had to be concealed, but how? He didn't have a bag or a coat. He shoved it up the front of his shirt until the point of the claw jabbed his neck, then tucked his shirt into his pants to hold the claw in place as he jogged to Mrs. Frost's.

They burst into Mrs. Frost's living room, startling the elderly woman as she leaned over her puzzle.

"Goodness, Berend. Is everything all right?"

He readjusted the claw beneath his shirt. "I really don't know."

"You're hurt," she said as she looked at his chin. Then her gaze lowered. "And there is something horribly wrong with your belly." She smiled at his bulging T-shirt.

"Yup." Bear untucked his shirt and slid out the giant lobster claw.

Her eyebrows shot up and her jaw dropped down. "Where did you get that?"

"I thought it could be part of a Halloween costume. I have another one at Gramma's."

She leaned forward and lowered her voice. "Berend, where did you get that?"

He tilted his head toward the golden retriever leaning against his leg.

"Honey? Honey the Wonder Dog got that?"

"Yup, and another one too."

"Come here, sweet girl." Mrs. Frost kissed the top of Honey's head. "You have a way of finding trouble."

"Why trouble? It's awesome. I didn't know they grew this big. Did you?"

Mrs. Frost took the claw from his hand and set it on top of her puzzle pieces. "This is evidence of a crime. You never see these because it's against the law. When a lobsterman catches a lobster this large, he's supposed to throw it back in the ocean, just like when he catches one too small or a female covered with eggs."

Bear fell back into the recliner and looked at the giant claw sitting between them.

"The rules are designed to protect the fisheries. There are big fines and you can even lose your lobster license if you're caught breaking them."

"That's why Hiram told us not to tell anyone," Bear gasped.

"What are we going to do with this?" Mrs. Frost looked nervous as she asked the question.

Bear squeezed his eyebrows together and thought. "I could smash it up and bury it in Gramma's compost pile." His hand reached for the lobster claw and he scattered puzzle pieces onto the floor.

Mrs. Frost gently placed her gnarled hand on top of his. "Berend, dear, that would be destroying evidence."

6

Sunday morning, Bear and Honey the Wonder Dog stood at the front window peering down Maple Street for the first sign of Olivia. Gauzy fog, dotted with swirling leaves, blew uphill with the winds off the ocean. It looked like a thick white curtain billowing across Maple Street and then retreating, revealing and then concealing the turn in the road. Bear could hear his grandmother humming in the kitchen as she cooked breakfast. The aroma of bacon tempted him, but he had to talk to Olivia before anyone else showed up. Honey saw her before Bear did and the dog's tail thumped against Bear's foot. They raced each other to the door. Honey was so intent on getting out that she blocked Bear. He bent over, wrapped his arms around her chest, and pulled the dog backwards across the well-worn wide-pine floorboards.

"Stay"—he thrust the palm of his hand in the golden retriever's face—"until I get the door open."

By the time they made it to the front porch, Olivia was already coming up the steps.

"Shh," Bear said as he held a finger in front of his mouth.

"I didn't say anything."

"Now you did."

"What?" Olivia plopped onto the porch steps. "What's the matter with you this morning?"

"We have to be quiet. I talked to Mrs. Frost..." This was hardly news. He talked to Mrs. Frost every day. "...about the lobster claws." With an exaggerated expression, he mouthed the words rather than saying them.

Olivia's brown eyes widened. "What?" She slapped a hand over her mouth before whispering, "Hi told us not to tell anyone."

"That's because," Bear paused and looked around to make sure no one was watching, "he's a criminal."

"You're crazy."

"No. It's true. Mrs. Frost told me. It's against the law to keep lobsters that big."

"We don't know he caught them." Olivia shook her head. "Do you have them? Both of them?"

Bear leaned toward Olivia's ear to whisper, "Hid them in my closet. I didn't want to destroy evidence."

"What are you two talking about?" Sally Parker startled them. They swung around and saw her wiping her hands on a dish towel.

They stared back silently. What had she heard?

"Our Halloween costumes?" Bear said, but it sounded like a question, not a statement.

"We want it to be a surprise," Olivia added.

"Come on. Come on. Get inside. Wash your hands. Your breakfast is getting cold." She looked at them suspiciously. "I thought you might be investigating another mystery. You're both natural detectives." Sally Parker chuckled. "Did someone steal your pumpkins?" She looked over her shoulder. "Nope, they're still there."

Relieved, Bear reached for the doorknob. His grandmother must not have heard their conversation.

"Buckaroo," she said, "what does Honey have in her mouth?"

Olivia and Bear stared at each other. "Not again!"

They looked down at the golden retriever behind them, her tail swishing through the air. She held something in her mouth. But it was different. Bear fell to his knees and held out his hand. Honey dropped a slimy, plump green apple into his palm. Bear exhaled as Olivia sagged against the door.

"Just an apple. Can she have it?"

"I wonder where that came from," his grandmother said. "Of course. Now wash your hands."

After breakfast, as the foghorns echoed across the bay, Olivia and Bear headed back to the front yard to count and sort their pumpkins. They knew they didn't have enough, and everyone on the island had already donated every pumpkin they could spare. The question was: How could they get more?

"What if the bottom row was basketballs?" Bear asked. "In the dark they would look like pumpkins."

"Do you think there are twenty-seven basketballs on the island?" Olivia asked. After a moment of silence, she whispered, "Could've been any one of the lobstermen." She grunted as she lifted an exceptionally large pumpkin.

"You heard him threaten us."

"Threaten us?"

"Yup. He said, 'Never tell anyone.'" Bear spoke with a menacing voice. "'If anyone ever finds out, you don't know the trouble you'll be in,'" he snarled, trying to imitate Hiram Wiley speaking around a pipe clenched in his teeth.

"Shh." Olivia reminded him to whisper. Sound carried in the fog and it was too thick for them to see if anyone was approaching. "He didn't say it like that." She started counting pumpkins. "We're short more than seventy." She stopped and looked at Bear. "It could be any one of the lobstermen." She pulled her short black hair away from her face. "Or more than one. Hi could be protecting someone else." Olivia put her hands on her hips and chewed on her lower lip. "Hi's a good guy. He brings us lobster meat sometimes. Remember, Alberta said they used to give away the ones that had thrown claws, that couldn't be sold. He brought them to us, my dad and me. Probably to others too. He never gave us a really big lobster like Honey found." The scrunching sound of car tires on the dirt road silenced her.

They peered down Maple Street. A silver minivan with a glowing taxi sign on its roof emerged from the fog. It came to a stop in Sally Parker's front yard.

"Did Zoe get a new taxi?" Bear asked.

Before Olivia could answer, Amiin Daahir waved at them from behind the steering wheel. Ubah jumped out and ran over to greet them.

"My father brought you something." Olivia and Bear leaned forward to hear the quiet words slipping from her delicate mouth. "Go. See. Go." She fluttered her hands toward the back of the taxi.

"My taxi has never been on a ferry before." Mr. Daahir's voice rose from the rear of the minivan. "We have a community garden," he added as they approached him, "and Somalis are excellent gardeners. As you can see."

When he stepped away from the taxi doors, Olivia and Bear gasped. Ubah hopped silently between them. The back seats had been removed from the van and it was full, wall to wall, floor to ceiling, with pumpkins of all shapes and sizes.

"A sincere thank you from our community to yours." Mr. Daahir spoke solemnly and Ubah stopped hopping. "For assisting my daughter. We are grateful. More than even pumpkins can suggest." His serious face evaporated into a grin bigger than Bear and Olivia's. "Where should we place them?"

When the pumpkins had all been unloaded and divided into groups based on height, everyone began counting. They needed 166 in all, but there also had to be the right number of same-sized pumpkins for each row. As Olivia moved pumpkins from one group to another, Bear lost count.

There was a break in the fog and Mrs. Frost's side window and front door opened simultaneously. The Professor stepped onto the porch as Mrs. Frost's head popped out the window and she hollered, "First adjust the pumpkins within each layer. Nine times three, that's twenty-seven pumpkins for the bottom row. You'll need twenty-four for the second row. Twenty-one for the third and so on. If you have enough for each row, then you'll know you have enough for your pyramid."

"And remember," the Professor added, "reserve a pumpkin exemplar for the peak of your pyramid."

The island's cherry-red taxi pulled up behind Mr. Daahir's taxi and Zoe hopped out. Her dreadlocks swayed from side to side with each step. Her flowing rust and maroon skirt was the perfect match for their fall activities.

"Dude," she joked as she gestured toward Mr. Daahir's taxi, "I don't think there's enough business out here for both of us."

"I am not competing. On your island, I transport only produce."

"I guess you do." Zoe turned in a circle, her skirt and hair swirling around her, to view all the pumpkins. "Totally awesome. Can I help?"

"We're just getting these sorted for the rows," Olivia said. "And to make sure we have enough. Then Dad said we should go to the fish house to help carry the rebar frame."

"It's too big for a car or a truck," Bear added. "And heavy. We'll need everybody."

They quickly finished the process of shifting pumpkins among their nine rows until the pumpkins in each row were as closely matched for size as possible.

"Four extras!" Olivia high-fived Bear.

He reached out for a fist bump before shouting, "Kaboom!"

"Let's get the metal frame."

Bear was not going to let Honey out of his sight. He had to make sure she didn't uncover any more evidence in front of all these people. Ubah, Olivia, and Bear strolled with the adults, sharing their excitement. The pumpkin pyramid was going to become a reality. As they walked past the bed and breakfast, a bank of fog blew by and they could see Victor and Hiram standing by the fish house, eagerly waving at them. The kids and Honey broke into a run, racing past Victor and Hiram to the ocean side of the shack. The two large doors were propped open. Their metal structure resembled a playground jungle gym.

"Wow!" They approached slowly, in awe, followed quietly by Victor and Hiram.

"Someone could live in this," Bear said.

His grandmother, Zoe, and Mr. Daahir appeared in the door.

"You followed the plans precisely," Mr. Daahir said to Victor and Hiram.

Their proud moment was interrupted by Sally Parker. "We have a long way to carry this beast." She walked around the large metal structure, staring at its peak, which rose above her head. "And it's uphill."

Hiram stepped forward. "Zoe, Amiin, and I can each take a corner." They moved to their appointed spots. "Let's see, Olivia, you're here. Bear and Ubah, you two get that side, and Sally can be over here." When everyone was in place, they looked at Hiram. "Victor'll tow the plywood behind his wheelchair."

Bear and Olivia exchanged glances.

"Plywood?" Bear asked.

"To stop the pumpkins from falling into the pyramid," Mr. Daahir explained, as he and Hiram carried three large plywood triangles out of the shed.

"Do you think that's a good idea?" Bear's grandmother followed Mr. Daahir and Hiram out of the shed.

Curious, Bear trailed them to the road. They attached a cart to the back of Victor's wheelchair and secured the plywood triangles upright in the cart, carefully balancing them to prevent the cart from falling on its side. When they were tied into place, they added a bright *Slow-Moving Vehicle* sign on the back of the cart. It looked like Victor was towing a sailboat down Water Street.

"Victor, that looks really heavy, and Wharf Street is awfully steep…" Sally Parker's voice trailed off.

"Can't weigh much more than a hundred pounds," Victor said. "It's not like I'm trying to pull a car up that hill." Bear's grandmother did not look convinced, but Victor moved on. "I'll go down the road in front of you, just in case there are any cars coming along. That should clear the way for you and the pyramid."

As Bear turned back toward the ocean and the fish house, Honey emerged from the fog at the water's edge. She had something in her mouth.

"Be right there," Bear hollered as he raced toward the dog. He chased her back into the fog before grabbing her collar and holding his hand beneath her mouth. "Drop it!" She deposited a tiny greenish-brown lobster, barely larger than his hand, in his palm. There were rubber bands loosely placed on the claws that kept it from pinching Bear and Honey. Bear was no lobsterman, but even he knew this little lobster was too small to be a keeper. He slid the rubber bands off and tossed the lobster into the ocean, hoping it would be all right. With a firm hand on Honey's collar, he walked back to the fish house. "Stay by my side. You hear me?"

Honey winked her response.

"Bear, come on," his grandmother called. "Everybody's waiting. We don't want to get stuck in boat traffic."

"Now you got me in trouble," he muttered at Honey as she raced toward the sound of her owner with her tail swishing high in the air.

"What a good girl," Sally Parker said as she looked into her dog's eyes.

Bear glared at the dog and took his place next to Ubah.

7

"Everybody set?" Hiram asked, exhaling nutty smoke from the corners of his thin lips. "On the count of three, we lift. If you feel wobbly, best speak up before we're walking." Everyone nodded their agreement. Bear marveled at how Hiram could speak with a pipe in his mouth. "One, two, three, lift."

Standing upright, Bear was relieved. The weight seemed manageable.

"Everybody okay?" Hiram asked.

"Yup!"

"Yes!"

"Totally!"

"Yeah!"

"Yes, sir!"

The enthusiastic answers jumbled together as they began walking into the fog of the fall day. They moved slowly as a determined group up the boat ramp to Water Street.

Rumbling and creaking through the fog, Bear heard the metal bridge for the car ferry lowering into place and knew that in a few minutes cars and people would be surging up Wharf Street. They had to get to the bed and breakfast before the cars driving off the ferry. Otherwise, their rebar pyramid would become stuck in the island's hourly traffic jam.

Hiram must have had the same thought. "A little faster." His voice was low and slow. "Little faster."

Gradually, silently, with their shoulders leaning into the metal skeleton, they responded and picked up their pace.

In front of them, Victor's arms bulged as he pushed on the wheels of his chair with renewed force. "I have to pick up speed to make it up the hill," he hollered over his shoulder. The trailer and plywood jerked behind him as he surged forward, gathering speed. The first car was driving slowly off the ferry. Victor would make it to the intersection of Wharf and Water streets before the cars got there. The pyramid might not. Bear grimaced at the thought of towing three sheets of plywood up Wharf Street's steep incline.

Bear watched Victor picking up speed, racing toward the intersection. The *Slow-Moving Vehicle* sign seemed like more of a joke now than when they had placed it on the cart. Bear's arms ached. Maybe it was the sight of Victor's flexed muscles thrusting him forward faster and faster toward the turn. Maybe it was the weight of the rebar pyramid. But there was no time to take a break and Bear did not want to be the one who was responsible for the group failing. They could not block the road with a pyramid when the ferry was unloading and loading. Horns would honk, neighbors would glare, and everyone would question their island etiquette. Bear knew all this, still he yearned for a break. They had to make it to Wharf Street. They had to make the turn. Keep moving forward. He and Honey had already slowed them enough.

Honey? Where was that dog? Bear quickly scanned the road. The golden retriever trotted proudly beside Sally Parker, oblivious to the trouble she had caused by delaying their start. Bear looked down the road toward Victor. A gust of wind coming off the water pushed a puff of fog past the stop sign. The vehicles from the ferry disappeared into a cloud of fog.

Rolling at top speed, Victor began to turn onto Wharf Street. The wind caught the large sheets of plywood as the trailer swung out behind Victor. The trailer made the turn and continued to circle, whipping around in an arc until it collided with Victor. He was ejected from his wheelchair and tossed into the road. Those who missed seeing Victor airborne turned when they heard the crash. Each car driving off the ferry slammed into the car it was following. The sounds of bumpers crumpling and horns blasting captured everyone's attention.

Olivia was the first to drop the pyramid. She ran and screamed, "Dad! Dad!" The metal structure crashed to the ground as the others stood in stunned silence.

Hiram Wiley spoke with a slow, booming tone. "Sally, run for Officer Calvin. Amiin and Zoe, let's get this out of the road." His voice was calm, but the urgency was clear. His pipe fell in the street as they struggled to move the pyramid onto the bed and breakfast's lawn.

Bear scooped up the pipe, worried that a car would crush it, before racing to Olivia's side.

Within minutes, Hiram Wiley was in the intersection of Wharf and Water streets directing traffic, clearing the way for the ambulance to attend to Victor.

When Officer Calvin and an EMT reached his side, Victor tried to wave them away. "It's just some scrapes and bruises," he said as his hands gingerly touched the bloody gash above his right eye. "I'll be fine."

Mr. Daahir examined Victor's wheelchair for damage as the EMT insisted on cleaning and bandaging Victor's injuries. They were now circled by other islanders walking up from the ferry, concerned about Victor and curious about the sheets of plywood in the road and the rebar pyramid on the lawn in front of the bed and breakfast.

"There is something you could do," Victor said.

"I have to check you for a concussion, and your wrist looks sprained—" the EMT began.

Victor cut him off. "Do you think that plywood would fit in the ambulance?" The crowd laughed. "No. Really. The hill's too steep for me."

The EMT put a butterfly bandage on Victor's head and stepped back. "We're not a delivery service." But it was too late. Mr. Mooney and Officer Calvin were loading the plywood triangles into the back of the ambulance as he spoke.

"Thanks a lot," Victor said to the confused EMT as Hiram and Mr. Daahir gently placed Victor in his wheelchair.

"We could use some volunteers," Hiram began, but there was no need. The metal framework was already being carried toward him as he spoke. Olivia pushed her father up the hill as Bear answered everyone's questions about the pumpkin pyramid. They made their way back to Sally Parker's house, following the ambulance with its siren and lights going for added effect. Bear knew that had to be Officer Calvin's decision.

Mrs. Frost and the Professor were standing on her front porch, drawn from the house by the ambulance's siren. Bear jogged over when he saw their concerned faces. The memories of the Professor's September ride in the ambulance were still fresh and terrifying. Bear didn't want his friends to worry.

"It's okay." He saw Mrs. Frost's thin, veiny arms quivering as she gripped her sides. "It's okay."

"Who is it? What happened?" Mrs. Frost leaned against the Professor. Her head trembled below his shoulder.

"It's okay." Bear pulled a rocking chair over and guided the ninety-year-old into the seat. "The plywood knocked Victor out of his wheelchair." At the sight of their confused faces, Bear continued. "I know. It was crazy. Like a sail in the wind. It just swung around and, Kapow! It knocked him in the air." Bear could see that his words weren't reassuring Mrs. Frost. "Really. He's okay. He's not in the ambulance." This was obvious, since Olivia was approaching them, pushing her father in his wheelchair as he held his right arm protectively against his chest.

Mrs. Frost's hands flew to her mouth. "Victor? You look…terrible. Bear said you were okay, but—"

"Dad needs a doctor," Olivia said. "He might have a concussion."

"No." Victor started to lift his hand in protest and grimaced. "Maybe it is sprained," he mumbled.

"Children, convey Victor to the porch. It's fortunate you built that wheelchair ramp for me," the Professor said as Olivia and Bear pushed Victor into place beside Mrs. Frost.

Mrs. Frost reached over to pat Victor's hand—the hand of the strongest man Bear knew. Victor had always seemed indestructible in spite of the wheelchair, or perhaps because of the wheelchair. Bear didn't know. He stared at the three adults on the porch. The Professor balanced precariously on his crutches as he brushed Victor's black hair away from the gash on his forehead. On the other side, Mrs. Frost appeared even smaller than usual. Her gnarled white hand, crisscrossed with veins, patted Victor Anaya's muscular brown hand. Victor sat slumped in his chair as they watched his wrist swell.

"Berend, Olivia, go on and help your friends. They won't know what to do without you," Mrs. Frost said.

"I—" Olivia began.

"We're here," was all Mrs. Frost said. Bear knew what she meant: they would take care of Olivia's father. But Olivia had always done that by herself and seemed reluctant to leave.

"It's okay," Bear said as he touched her arm. He had to stop saying that. Olivia didn't look like she believed him, and he knew he didn't believe himself. "Mrs. Frost and the Professor know what to do."

Olivia managed to nod her head as they turned to join their neighbors in front of his grandmother's house. The bustling, joking crowd didn't seem concerned about Victor Anaya's injuries. Like Bear, they must be relying on his reputation for overcoming any challenge. But Bear had seen Victor slouching and Olivia's response. They were worried.

Mr. Daahir walked toward them. "I must return my taxi to service on the other side of the bay. I hope to see photos of your exceptionally large pumpkin pyramid."

"Wait," Sally Parker said. "I have something for Ubah and Olivia." She went inside.

"How is your father?" Mr. Daahir asked as he looked past Olivia and Bear toward the quiet cluster on Mrs. Frost's porch.

"His wrist's swollen. He thinks it's sprained," Olivia said.

"Can he push his wheels?"

Olivia shook her head. Bear looked at Olivia's and Mr. Daahir's serious expressions. A sprained wrist meant Victor couldn't move his wheelchair. Bear sucked air through his teeth. Victor not moving, stuck, stationary was impossible to imagine.

"Ubah, come here." His grandmother interrupted their gloomy thoughts and Ubah ran over to join them. "You two have a big meet this Friday. I thought you could use some new shoes. Racing flats!" She held out a pair toward each girl. Try them tomorrow at practice. If they don't fit, I can exchange them before the meet."

Olivia and Ubah were speechless as they looked at the new shoes. Bear knew it had been a long time since Olivia had received a pair of shoes that weren't just new to her but brand new. Based on the look on Ubah's face, he suspected she had been wearing other people's cast-offs for a long time too.

"Thank you." Olivia hugged Bear's grandmother.

"They are perfect," Ubah whispered shyly to the shoes.

Mr. Daahir nodded his thanks and shook Sally Parker's hand. For several moments he looked around the yard and at the trio on Mrs. Frost's porch before he was able to speak. "For many years, I have dreamed of a place like this, but I never believed it could be more than a dream." With a final solemn nod, he and Ubah returned to the taxi and the short ferry ride back to Portland.

8

After Mr. Daahir and Ubah drove down the road to get his taxi in line for the next ferry, Bear tugged on Olivia's arm. He had to talk to her when no one else could hear him.

"Stop tugging on me." She glared.

"It's important," Bear whispered. "Honey got another one."

Olivia shook her head and then arched her black eyebrows as she made peculiar little gestures with her hands.

"What?"

Without moving her lips, she mumbled, "Behind you."

"What?" This time he forgot to whisper. A tap on Bear's shoulder from Hiram Wiley instantly explained all of Olivia's gestures.

"Hey, Hi," Olivia and Bear said in unison.

Bear's fake smile made the muscles in his face cramp,

but Hiram just stared at them and puffed on the pipe that Bear had rescued from the road.

Finally, he spoke. "This here's my wife, Flo." He jerked his thumb toward the stern-looking woman at his side. "She's a nurse. Retired."

"Nurse practitioner." She corrected her husband with a clipped precision that he appeared to ignore.

"Thought your dad might like a second opinion." Hiram looked at his wife, took the pipe out of his mouth, and smiled. Bear began to relax, just a little.

"Maybe," Olivia said hesitantly. "Wait a second." She ran across the yard to the porch, where her father was sitting silently between the Professor and Mrs. Frost.

Bear nervously looked back and forth between Hiram and Flo, unsure of what he should say. He didn't want to ask about lobsters in case he revealed too much, but he was having a hard time keeping his thoughts to himself. "Hey, Hi," Bear looked at his feet. "How big does a lobster have to be to keep it?"

"Three and a quarter to five inches."

Bear held his index fingers out and moved them apart, together, apart, guessing at the distance.

Hiram reached out and grabbed Bear's hands in his huge mitts. Bear stepped backward but his hands were imprisoned. "Here to here," Hiram said as he moved Bear's hands, indicating the legal size.

"That's really small," Bear said when Hiram released his hands.

There was a low sound in Hiram's throat that might have been laughter. "That's just the carapace."

"Carapace?"

"Body. Not the tail. Not the claws."

Olivia was back. "Dad said yes."

Flo Wiley turned and strode across the lawn. She was carrying a medical bag. Her husband followed a few steps behind her.

For the first time in hours, Olivia and Bear were the only people in the front yard, surrounded by pumpkins. Bear looked around one more time to make sure it was safe to talk. The fog was gone. The dog was gone. "Where's Honey?" What would that dog bring home this time? With the Wileys next door! Without the fog, there was no chance of concealing anything hanging out the sides of her mouth.

"Your gramma took her in."

Bear exhaled like a popped balloon. When his heart rate slowed, he spoke. "She got another one, but this time it was too small and still alive. I took the rubber bands off the claws and threw it back in the ocean."

"Someone banded a lobster that was too small?" Olivia looked like she didn't believe him. "Do you even know the lobster regulations?"

Bear stood up straight, squared his shoulders, and looked directly at Olivia's brown eyes. "Three and a quarter to five inches long for the…" What was the word Hiram had said? "For the…for the body."

"Carapace?" Olivia smiled.

"Yup. That's right. The carapace has to be between three and a quarter and five inches. That doesn't include the tail or the claws."

"I know." Olivia shook her head. "How big was the one Honey got?"

Bear moved his hands closer, then further apart, then a little closer together.

"A dollar bill's six inches. Was it bigger or smaller than that?"

"A little bigger than a dollar bill."

"Take away the tail and claws…that has to be too small. Not even close. How much meat could there be?" Olivia seemed to be talking to herself.

"Imagine getting that tail in a restaurant." Bear laughed at the thought of a large dinner plate with a tiny lobster tail in the middle. "Or two scrawny little claws."

"It doesn't make sense." Olivia dragged one of the plywood triangles over to the metal pyramid. "That was really nice of your grandmother to get me those shoes." She put another sheet of plywood in place. "Makes me feel like I have to run."

Bear helped Olivia adjust the third triangle. They attached them to the frame with ties from the colorful twine Hiram used for crocheting bait bags. Bear thought about what she had said. Did it mean she might not run? She had been grouchy ever since her dad got hurt, so he had to pick his words carefully. "Are you thinking—" he began slowly.

Olivia waved his words away and then went to grab one of the biggest pumpkins and place it against the plywood. "We need a plan for catching whoever's keeping those illegal lobsters."

"Yup." He followed her with another large pumpkin for the bottom row. "Shouldn't we carve them first?"

Olivia stared at him.

"Before we put them in place. It doesn't make sense to stack them and then unstack them and then—"

"We can't carve a hundred and sixty-six pumpkins."

"Why not? We didn't think we could get a hundred and sixty-six pumpkins and we did."

"If we carve them, they'll rot and turn to goo."

Bear sat down on a large pumpkin. "Really?" He picked at the stem.

Olivia pulled over a pumpkin and sat down across from him. She leaned forward and said, "We should keep our costumes secret. I have the best idea."

Bear looked up. "Really?"

"I'll be a lobster trap and you can be a lobster."

He liked the idea. He liked it so much it erased most of his disappointment about not being able to have a carved and lit pumpkin pyramid. "You can chase me and catch me. Trap me!" Bear said eagerly.

Olivia shook her head and wiped her forehead. "That's not how lobsters are caught. You know that, right? The traps don't chase—"

"I know," Bear said. "Of course, I know." Sometimes she acted like he was a total idiot. "It was a joke."

Olivia scooted closer on her pumpkin until their knees were touching and leaned forward.

"It has to be one of the lobstermen."

Bear jumped up. "I know lobstermen catch lobsters. I know traps don't chase them." With each sentence his voice was louder. "I'm not an idiot."

Olivia looked confused. The adults on Mrs. Frost's porch were staring at them.

"Sit down," she hissed and gestured toward his pumpkin seat. "What's wrong with you?"

Bear slumped onto his pumpkin.

"We have to find where they're burying the lobster shells," Olivia said. "Where is Honey getting the claws? It has to be one of the lobstermen. That narrows our list of suspects. If we find where they dump the shells, then that's the spot we watch."

Now she had his attention. "Maybe Mrs. Claus," he touched the Band-Aid on his chin to indicate he meant Alberta Goodhue, "can help us. She must see what the lobstermen bring in. What they take out. Or do you think Hiram told us not to say anything because he and his son are responsible?"

Before Olivia could answer, Bear's grandmother called from the porch. "Kids?" Honey trotted over to greet them. "I thought I could make lobster mac and cheese for everyone for dinner." Sally Parker gestured toward Mrs. Frost's porch, where Flo Wiley was putting something on Victor's wrist while Hiram measured the wheelchair and made notes on a pad of paper. "We'll eat at Viola's." Whenever Victor Anaya came to dinner, they ate at Mrs. Frost's. "Can you two run down to the fish house and get some lobster meat for me?"

"The fish house? They sell lobster meat?" Bear asked.

"That woman, Alberta Goodhue, she's the cleaning lady at the bed and breakfast—"

"We met her."

"Yesterday."

"Isn't she sweet? Reminds me of Mrs. Claus with her white hair and round rosy cheeks," Sally Parker said. "Two pounds should be enough." She handed money to Bear. "Do you want to take Honey?" The golden retriever wagged her tail and looked up at them expectantly.

"No-o-o!" Olivia and Bear blurted in unison, before glancing over at Viola Frost's front porch to see if anyone had heard them.

Honey sat and looked up at Bear with such sad eyes, he said, "Well, okay. But she has to be on a leash."

Before his grandmother could question Bear's sudden insistence on using a leash, Olivia said, "I'll run inside and get it."

Bear bent over to whisper to Honey. "You have to stay with us. If you see something suspicious, show us later. Don't run all over the island with it."

Honey stared back at him and wagged her tail in agreement. Then one eyebrow lifted slowly. Bear wasn't sure he could trust her.

9

Bear, Olivia, and Honey walked slowly down Wharf Street, heads leaning toward each other, voices lowered. Could they trust Alberta Goodhue? Should they trust Alberta Goodhue? Bear was sure she had the answers to all their questions, but Olivia didn't like her.

"She seemed nice enough at first. But when she said that about Frank, that he's persnickety-pickety—I don't know. Seemed…weird. He's a really good guy. We could ask her some questions but—"

"Don't let her know what we know."

"Exactly."

"Whoa!"

"What?"

Bear pointed toward the intersection of Wharf and Water streets. Two horses with riders stood in the middle of the road. The sun, sitting low in the sky, gave them a mysterious glow from behind. "Good thing Honey's on leash." He pulled the golden retriever a little closer to his legs.

"She's fine. They know each other. That's the harbor master and her daughter. Betty and Liz Bucknam. They keep their horses in the barn by our house. They only ride downtown when there isn't any traffic."

"Imagine going trick-or-treating on a horse. That would be so ni-i-ice." Bear stretched the last word. The horses' backs were head-high for him. He stared up at the riders sitting on the massive animals. "Hard to get your candy. You'd have to reach way down..." His voice trailed off as he wondered how hard it would be to ride a horse and carry a bucket full of candy. Maybe the horse could carry the candy.

"Before we get the lobster meat," Olivia said, interrupting his thoughts, "let's see if we can find where Honey got those lobster claws. We can sneak through the tall grass."

"What if I let Honey off—"

"We can follow her." Olivia nodded approval and grinned.

"But we can't let her out of our sight. No matter what!"

Honey and the horses appeared not to notice each other as she trotted behind the two large muscular animals standing calmly in the middle of the road. The harbor master and her daughter sat silent and still as they watched the sun slide toward Portland's skyline across the bay. The horses and riders could have been statues. Bear paused to stare, waiting for a whinny or a flick of a tail. The shiny black horse closest to him turned his head ever so slightly and stared into Bear's eyes with such intensity that Bear stepped backwards and raised his hands slightly in a half apology.

"Bear!" Olivia gestured for him to catch up. "You just said not to let Honey out of our sight."

Bear ran to catch up with her. He looked down Water Street and saw the back of Alberta Goodhue. She must have been talking to someone behind the fish house. The index finger on her right hand stabbed the air in front of her. Honey disappeared into the rugosa roses that edged the beach, and Bear and Olivia quietly followed her. When the fish house was between them and Alberta Goodhue, Bear put the leash back on Honey. They stopped, crouched down in the tall grass, and examined the beach in front of them. The rush of the waves on the incoming tide made it impossible to hear Alberta Goodhue.

Bear held Honey's face in his hands and looked into her eyes. "I'm going to let you off leash. Don't get too far ahead. Don't get into trouble. Please," he pleaded with the earnest-looking dog, who winked in response. "Lead us to the lobster claw graveyard," he whispered into her ear as he unhooked her leash.

With her tail waving above her back and head held high, Honey trotted out of the grass and onto the sandy beach. She paused to look side to side and cocked her head when she reached the line of seaweed at the high-tide mark. With her nose close to the sand, she took a few steps away from the ocean before diving into a digging stance and throwing sand into the air.

"No!" Bear hollered as he raced from their hiding place in the tall grass edging the beach. At the sound of his own voice, he clapped his hands over his mouth, hunched over, and hurried as quickly as an awkward boy strug-gling to hide on an open beach could. When he reached Honey, he flattened himself on the sand, grabbed her col-lar, and tried to pull her down to the ground beside him. "I told you—"

She licked his face. Bear rolled away, giggling, but Honey stood over him and nudged him with her nose. "Stop," he said, laughing, as he tried to sit up.

That's when he saw feet. Bear choked on his laughter. Feet in dirty, smelly shoes, in front of his face. These were not Olivia's feet. Bear's eyes scanned up the stained jeans. Was that the slimy green gunk from inside a lobster stick-ing to his right knee? Bear raised his eyes farther. From this angle he could see the man's hairy belly pushing his shirt away from the waistband of his pants.

"Whatcha doing?" The voice was not unfriendly.

Bear rose up on his knees, one arm around Honey's neck. Where was Olivia? Without turning his head, he glanced to the side. She was still hiding in the grass, gesturing wildly at Bear. His focus returned to the man in front of him. Bear was at eye level with the stranger's belly. A button was missing from the man's shirt and a tuft of belly hair stuck out through the gap. Bear thought about tucking it back inside but resisted the urge.

"Whatcha doing?" the man repeated. "Your dog's some digger." He had stepped away from Bear and was absentmindedly kicking sand back into the hole Honey had dug.

Bear tried to see if there were lobster shells in the rapidly filling pit.

"You need help getting up?"

"No. No." Bear hopped to his feet and started wiping sand off himself. "I'm fine. Thanks." Bear turned to the strange man and struggled not to stare at the gap in his shirt. The man had all of his fingers, so it seemed unlikely that he was a lobsterman. Plus, his hands were normal man-sized. And he wasn't a loud talker like so many of the island lobstermen, who had spent a lifetime yelling over the sound of their boat engines.

Olivia appeared at Bear's side. "Hi. I'm Olivia."

"Wayne." He crossed his arms over his chest, resting them on his belly. "I'm visiting my mom." He uncrossed his arms long enough to point toward Alberta Goodhue, who was standing by the fish house waggling her fingers and waving at them.

"Olivia! Bear!" Her sweet lilting voice called out. "How's your chin healing?"

"Your mom looks like Mrs. Claus," Bear said to Wayne as they all walked up the beach toward the fish house. She was beaming at them and wiping her hands on the dirty apron tied around her waist.

Wayne shook his head. "Don't think so."

Olivia elbowed Bear. Was it rude to say someone's mother looked like Mrs. Claus? He thought it was a compliment, but Wayne didn't seem to agree. Olivia elbowed him again. Bear's head snapped toward her and he mouthed, "What?"

She whispered, "Honey? Where's Honey?"

Not again. Bear reached into his pocket and took out the money his grandmother had given them. He shoved it into Olivia's hand. He made small hand motions at his side, hidden from Wayne, that he hoped would communicate *Distract them while I get Honey.* Olivia raised her eyebrows and twisted her mouth.

Bear spoke loudly. "Darn it. I forgot something. Be right back." He turned and took two steps away from Olivia and Wayne, hoping an idea would come to him. Where was that dog? And what would she be carrying when he found her? He scanned the beach. Sand was flying out from beneath the Lobstermen's Pier. He hoped no one else could see it. Trying not to attract anyone's attention, he walked as quickly as he dared toward the sandstorm. When he was sure he was out of sight of Alberta and Wayne Goodhue, he spotted Honey and ran to her side. There in the dark, damp sand under the pier, hidden from view, was the lobster shell graveyard and a very happy, sandy golden retriever. Bear stared into the pit she had created. It wasn't just sand flying past his head.

"Wait. Wait. Wait," Bear said. He picked up a giant lobster tail and a crusher claw.

Honey stopped and looked at him, tipping her head and raising one ear.

"Come here." At the sound of Bear's voice, Honey came and sat beside him. "We have to fill this in. If we leave a big pit, they'll know that we know." Bear turned his back to the hole, bent over, and started flinging sand between his legs like a dog. "Come on. Help me out." And with that, Honey turned and imitated Bear, tossing sand between her legs back into the air. Once she was moving the sand in the right direction, Bear circled the pit, tossing the lobster shells in before pushing more sand on top.

"That looks pretty good." He paused to wipe the sand off himself and Honey before snapping the leash on her collar. "Act like nothing happened." He took two steps out from under the pier toward the fish house before realizing it would be better not to be seen coming from the direction of the lobster graveyard. They pulled back, went under the pier and toward a steep hill on the other side. "I don't know." Bear looked up. From this angle it appeared to be a cliff, not a hill.

He glanced toward Honey. Above her head he saw a tree growing sideways, roots exposed, clinging to the cliff's face. When he joined her, he could see a path angling off to the side. Honey began climbing as Bear grabbed a bare root. When Honey's hind legs slipped on the eroding path, he pushed the dog's rear end until she pulled herself onto a ledge above the tree. Bear grabbed some wild roses to keep from sliding back into the ocean as he joined Honey on the narrow ledge. He steadied himself and tried to pick the thorns out of the palms of his hands.

His head was just above the precipice. When he stood on his tiptoes and gripped the crumbling cliff's edge, he saw seven tombstones, cracked and covered with lichen. They appeared to lean away from each other as if having an afterlife argument. Bear glanced toward Honey to make sure she was sitting in a safe spot before peering at the headstones. He could read the inscription on only one of them:

CHESTER FROST
BELOVED SON
1910–1919

Bear dropped below the cliff's edge and wrapped an arm around Honey's neck. He whispered into her furry ear, "He was younger than me." Slowly, he rose to his feet. "Only nine years old." Bear shook his head. "We gotta get out of here."

Honey waved her tail before squeezing her body between Bear and the cliff's edge. "Careful," Bear said as he grabbed for a tree root and turned to follow the golden retriever on her path through thorn bushes and shifting rocks. When he finally stood on the wide lawn surrounding the Seafarers Museum, the headstones seemed less eerie, nestled beneath a tree overlooking the ocean. He paused to catch his breath before jogging to the road. He had to get back to Olivia at the fish house.

"Hey, did you get the lobster meat?" Bear tried to sound normal when he saw Olivia with Wayne and Alberta Goodhue.

Olivia raised her eyebrows with an unasked question. "Yup. Ready to go home?"

"Yeah. Yeah." The Goodhues stared at Bear. Was he still covered in sand? Keep moving, he thought. Just act normal. "See you," he said as he turned and began running toward home.

When they had passed the bed and breakfast, he stopped to talk to Olivia. "Did you ask them any questions? See anything unusual? That Wayne guy's strange. Don't you think?"

"Where was Honey? You know you have sand...everywhere? I mean all over...everything?" She gestured up and down. "Did she get another claw?"

"We—she—found the graveyard. It's under the pier. She dug it all up but then we filled it back in again so no one would know. It's huge."

"Good work." She put her hand up for a high five and then a fist-bump kaboom.

"And I found a real graveyard by the Seafarers Museum."

"Yeah. That's an old one." Olivia wasn't impressed. "We better hurry home for dinner. They're going to wonder what took so long. But first, you have to clean up. You're both a mess."

Honey plopped onto her back in the middle of Wharf Street and Olivia did her best to rub the sand off her wet belly while Bear started at the top of his head, running his fingers through his brown curls, wiping the grit off his face, and scratching the back of his neck before brushing the sleeves of his shirt. "How do I look?"

"Turn around." Olivia came over and swiped her hand across his back with such force it knocked him a step up the hill with each cleansing thwap. "Good to go."

Dinner was Bear's favorite meal with his favorite people, and they were all in a good mood. Olivia was right: even the adults were excited about Halloween.

The Professor seemed the least likely to put on a disguise, but he had a plan. "Your preparations are infectious," he said to Olivia and Bear as they passed the lobster macaroni and cheese. "I have a plan. Top secret. Highly classified costume." He paused and looked around the table. "But I may need to borrow a few items in the coming days."

"Really?" Mrs. Frost looked surprised, and it is hard to surprise someone who has lived for nine decades. "I have a little something up my sleeve as well."

Bear looked, but all he saw up her sleeves were skinny, blotchy arms.

"Bear," she said. Had she noticed him staring at her arms? "After dinner can you get my sewing machine down from the attic and check to see what fabric I have up there?"

"Sure," he answered through a mouthful of pasta, relieved by the request. Was Mrs. Frost going trick-or-treating? She had a little smile on her face as she looked down at her food, a sure sign that she was scheming. The image of the boy's headstone at the top of the cliff flashed into Bear's head. "Mrs. Frost, did you have a brother? Chester?"

She shook her head sadly. "Oh, no. That was my husband's brother. He died in the 1918 flu pandemic. Clarence, my husband, was born after the pandemic. Four older brothers and sisters died before he was born. They're buried along with anyone else from the island who died from that flu. I don't know how many it was. Some families put up gravestones years later." Mrs. Frost looked at Bear. "But not everyone got a headstone.

Some families didn't have the money. Sometimes, everyone in the family died, and there was no one left to mark their graves. Everyone had to be buried within twenty-four hours to keep that terrible disease from spreading." She sighed. "And there weren't enough caskets..." Her voice faded away.

Bear looked at Olivia. She had seen the graveyard before, but even she looked shocked by what Mrs. Frost had said. Bear slid his plate away from him and extended his foot under the table, reaching for the comfort of Honey the Wonder Dog.

"I'm sorry," Mrs. Frost said, forcing a smile. "That's hardly appropriate dinner table conversation." Her head drooped and the smile faded.

After several minutes, Victor broke the silence. "Flo says my wrist is sprained. It will be weeks or longer before it's strong enough to wheel me around."

Someone gasped and there was a murmur. "Oh, no."

With his good arm, he waved away their concern. "Hiram is making a motor for my wheelchair. Once that's done, I'll be able to get around on my own again."

Bear was relieved by the new topic of conversation.

"We saw horses," Bear blurted. "Down by the gift shop."

Everyone nodded, unimpressed.

Victor leaned forward and asked, "Sawhorses or seahorses?"

"We saw horses," Bear repeated. Frustrated, he looked to Olivia for support.

She was grinning. "It's a joke. A dad joke. Get it? A saw-horse for cutting wood or—"

"Ooooh," Bear said with a mixture of embarrassment and humor. He ducked his head and took another bite, smiling at the play on words.

They had accomplished a lot in one weekend: they had all their pumpkins, the framework for the pyramid had been built and delivered, and they knew where the lobster graveyard was, thanks to Honey, who was sound asleep on his feet. Sunday supper always meant the end of the weekend. Normally, he would have to rush to finish his homework and chores before Monday morning. Tonight, he could relax and enjoy his friends.

Bear turned to Olivia. "Are you going back to school tomorrow?" he asked without thinking. She kicked him hard under the table, glared, and dipped her head one time.

10

Bear was slow to get up on Monday. It was supposed to be a school day, but it wasn't as if he had to finish any homework or race for the school bus. After breakfast he grabbed Honey's leash, but his grandmother placed a hand on his arm. She was shaking her head *no*.

"What? What? She'll have fun." Bear knew he would have more fun if she came with him. He didn't want to roam the island alone. Without thinking, he put the leash behind his back.

His grandmother looked at him sternly. "I don't know what the two of you did yesterday, but I'm still picking seaweed off her belly. She's staying home today and I'm giving her a bath and a thorough brushing. I swear you two brought home half the beach with you."

Bear was disappointed, but she was right, and he did not want to have to explain anything about Honey's detective-digging in the lobster graveyard. He hung the leash back on its hook in the mudroom and backed up toward the door before she could ask him how Honey had gotten so dirty. "I'll be gone at least four hours. I can't run with the samples in glass jars. And when I get home, I'll have to do pH tests." Maybe his grandmother would help him. Ms. Alcott, his teacher, had explained how the test strips would measure whether the water was acidic or basic, but Bear hadn't understood half of what she'd said.

"Love you." She ruffled his hair. "Have fun."

Honey whimpered quietly as she watched Bear reach for the doorknob.

"Sorry, girl. I can't."

His first stop was Mooney's Market. Bear needed snacks for his walk around the island gathering water samples and measuring the salinity and temperature of the ocean. He stepped through the double doors and was greeted by Mike Mooney, who stood with his arms crossed.

"Uh-oh. This does not look good. Don't tell me you did it again." Mr. Mooney's head hung down and shook sadly from side to side as he stared at Bear. "Buddy, you have got to—"

"I'm not in trouble!" Why did he have to keep explaining? Why was everyone so quick to forget all the good he'd done when he was on the island in September? He had been a hero.

Mr. Mooney's face broke into a grin as he patted Bear on the back. "Calm down. I already heard all about your *Guinness* record-setting pumpkin pile up."

"Then why—"

"A guy's gotta have a little fun, right?" Mr. Mooney leaned against the checkout counter and gestured around his empty store. "Slow time of year. I've been hearing a lot of good things about your project. The whole island is even more excited about Halloween than they usually are. I didn't think that was possible."

"What about you? What are you going to be for Halloween?"

Mr. Mooney's stern expression returned. "Do I look like the kind of person who puts on a silly costume and prances through the streets asking for candy? Really, Bear." Mr. Mooney walked away, shaking his head.

Olivia had told him that everybody—kids, grown-ups, even dogs—dressed up for Halloween. Obviously, she was wrong.

With a week's worth of snacks, five canning jars, a hydrometer, thermometer, rope, and notebook all stuffed in his backpack, Bear headed down Club Road toward his first stop, the Tennis and Yacht clubs. They closed at the end of September so no one should be there to notice if he used the long pier for gathering samples. The nets had been removed from the tennis courts. All of the large, shiny sailboats were gone. They were pulled from the ocean each fall, sanded, painted, and polished before they were set back in the sea again before Memorial Day. The only boats bobbing in the water were tiny and needed several coats of paint. Dinghies, skiffs, rowboats, dories, tenders—the islanders used all those words for the small wooden vessels in the ocean. But Bear couldn't tell the difference between the boats or the words. They seemed too basic to even have differences. He wasn't sure he would willingly head out in the ocean in any of these small and battered boats, barely bigger than buckets.

Bear had planned to study the density of seawater by measuring how salty and cold it was. He wanted to know if the water at the bottom of the ocean was colder and saltier than the water at the surface—or was it the other way around? He planned to check at five different places around the island and then test the pH of a water sample from each of the five spots. There were three long piers on the island extending into the bay, making it easier to drop his thermometer and hydrometer into deeper water.

It wasn't until he reached the end of the Yacht Club pier that he realized the ramp and float that were connected to it in the summer had been removed. There was nothing in front of him but the ocean, and that was at least eight feet below him. He sat and looked around. All the wooden boats were tied to a float beside the pier. There must be a ladder, some way to get down there, but he couldn't see it. He stared down. The water might be twenty feet deep. He lay down at the end of the pier, thinking he could drop the thermometer from there, but he didn't have enough rope to reach the water plus twenty feet below the surface. How would he get a water sample?

As he unpacked his sample jars and notebook, a bald eagle soared above him, its white head flashing in the sunlight. Bear heard the crows *cawing* before he saw them. They were chasing the eagle, taking turns swooping down toward the eagle's back. The majestic eagle dipped and turned to evade the crows' assaults. The crows looked puny compared to the eagle, but the bigger bird made no attempt to attack the three black birds that were harassing him. Bear laughed at the sight of the smaller black birds working together, chasing the eagle away from shore. Were they protecting a nest?

Bear managed to tie his rope around a canning jar and drop it into the ocean. Water sloshed out of the jar as he pulled it back up, but it was over half full when he screwed on the lid. He labeled his first jar of sea water and then attached the thermometer to the rope. He would drop it as far into the water as he could. It wasn't perfect, but what choice did he have?

His backpack was a little heavier as he headed toward the starfish pools. If it was close to low tide, he would see starfish, periwinkles, mussels and crabs in the seawater that filled the cracks and indentations in the rocks along the shore. Bear walked down the middle of the road past empty summer homes. The water in the jar sloshed with each step. Even the caretakers were gone. In the summer, cars would be zipping past, families playing in the large grassy yards, landscapers mowing lawns, and you could smell grills, BBQ smokers, and fire pits every day. But today the sights, sounds, and smells were all natural and were his alone. A leaf drifted down and Bear leapt to catch it. The sudden clanking of glass in his backpack reminded him not to jump around.

A wave broke on the rocks. The tide was too high. He wouldn't be able to see starfish this morning. They lived in the tidepools closest to the low tide line, immersed in the chilly ocean all day. The higher tide might make it easier to get temperatures at deeper depths. Bear hadn't considered the tides. Should he take all his measurements at high tide, low tide, or mid-tide? Would it make a difference in the temperature, density, or salinity? He didn't know when high tide was, but right now it looked high, mostly. All the barnacles and mussels were under water. But was it incoming or outgoing? Being a scientist was a lot more complicated than he had expected. Every question led to five more.

Bear sat down, opened his backpack, and pulled out a package of Goldfish crackers. If Olivia were with him, she would help him sort this out. Or Mrs. Frost. She always had the answers and a practical approach to any problem. The three of them together were like those crows chasing away the bigger, stronger bald eagle. And if Honey were with him? He'd probably be struggling to pull her out of the water and over the rocks, which were covered with slippery seaweed. He smiled at the thought.

When the crackers were gone, he pulled out the hydrometer Ms. Alcott had loaned him, put his backpack on, and went out on the rocks. He could easily get a sample of water from a tide pool, but he wanted something deeper where the dark rocks hadn't been warming in the sun for hours. Bear looked for a place with a steep drop-off so he could check the water at least ten feet below the surface. Twenty would be better. With each step there was more slippery seaweed covering the rocks. He slowed, trying to find secure footing on bare stone.

The crashing sound of a wave breaking on the rocks in front of him forced Bear to look up. An even bigger wave came straight at him from behind it. He took two steps backwards and felt his feet slip forward as his head flew back. The next crashing sound might have been the wave that broke over his legs or the sample jars that broke beneath his back. It was hard to know. But as he lay on the rocks staring up at the sky, the waves kept crashing.

When he felt ice-cold water flowing around his knees, he pushed himself up and retreated. His pants were soaked. His grandmother's canning jars were smashed. The first sample dripped from his backpack and the notebook was drenched. He had no choice but to return to his grandmother's house for dry clothes, more sample jars, and a break. Bear needed time to think.

As he walked past the Yacht and Tennis clubs, he glanced toward the small wooden boats swaying in the water. From a distance, they almost appeared seaworthy. There had to be a better way to get his measurements than slipping and falling on the rocks. He could stick to the west side of the island and give up on getting any samples from the backshore. But he was curious about the eastern side and the open ocean. The waves were bigger; was the water also colder, saltier? He wanted to measure the things he couldn't see.

After Bear cleaned the broken glass out of his backpack and changed his clothes, he joined his grandmother and the Professor for lunch at Mrs. Frost's house.

In between bites of his sandwich he explained about slipping on the rocks, losing his first sample and all of the canning jars.

"I need more canning jars. Do you think I could just measure the tide pools on the backshore? That seems wrong. They'd all be warmer, wouldn't they? Anywhere I go I'll have the same problem trying to get to the deep water. I could just take measurements off the three piers on the island. I don't know. I don't know what to do."

"The person to ask is Hiram Wiley," Bear's grandmother said.

"I don't know." Bear didn't want to reveal his suspicions. "There's something about him…"

"Why, Berend, he's the salt of the earth," Mrs. Frost said.

"Is that a good thing?"

The Professor took over. "One of the brightest minds I've ever encountered."

"Honest as the day is long," Mrs. Frost added.

"You two are like the Riddler. Really." Bear sounded frustrated.

Mrs. Frost smiled. "Let's keep it simple. You want help. He's your man."

"Speaking of help," the Professor said, "do either of you have a slip I could borrow?"

Bear's grandmother and Mrs. Frost burst out laughing and raised their hands to their mouths in surprise.

"What's a slip?" Bear asked.

"Women used to wear them under dresses or skirts—"

"All I require is the version that drapes from the waist to the knees. Not excessively lacy. Preferably white."

The two women shook their heads, obviously amused. "You're a lot bigger than we are."

"What do you need it for?" Bear asked.

"That, my young friend, is top secret."

"I'm outta here," Bear said as he rose to leave. The last thing he wanted to talk about was slips. Still, as he walked toward the fish house, he couldn't help but wonder why the Professor was interested in women's underwear.

11

Bear smelled the pipe smoke as soon as he was in front of the bed and breakfast. Hiram Wiley must be at the fish house. Olivia always said: *You do the hardest things first. That way when you're tired you just have the easy stuff left.* Talking to that old lobsterman would be the hardest thing. But everyone said Hiram Wiley could help him, and if that were true then everything would be easier.

Bear left the sidewalk and slipped through the roses and deep beach grass, trying to get to the Lobstermen's Pier without seeing or being seen by the old man. It wasn't Bear who made the decision to avoid Hiram. His feet made it for him, and he just followed. "Nope. Not doing it," they said with each step.

When he hit the open beach, he moved quickly toward the Lobstermen's Pier, deliberately avoiding looking back at the fish house. He hoped Hiram Wiley was preoccupied with crocheting bait bags, mending traps, or painting lobster buoys and wouldn't see him. Bear glanced down through the creaky pier boards and saw the lobster graveyard just above the high-tide line. Whoever tried to hide the shells here must have been worried the ocean would pull the sand away and reveal them if they were buried any lower on the beach.

Just like at the Yacht Club, the ramps and floats extending farther into the ocean had been removed for the winter. Standing high above a float secured to the side of the pier, Bear held on to a piling and leaned outward. From this angle he could see the vertical ladder attached to the side of the pier, practically beside him. He climbed down the ladder to the float. From here, Bear was hidden by the pier pilings, but he could spy around them and see Hiram Wiley. When he lay on his belly to see how deep the water was, he glanced toward the fish house. Hiram Wiley sat in a chair, tipped back against the building, baseball cap pulled down over his eyes and pipe dangling from his mouth. Was he sleeping?

Bear took out his thermometer, which was attached to a rope with markings at ten and twenty feet. He lowered it into the water until the thermometer was completely submerged. He watched the second hand on his watch as it circled the dial. After a minute he pulled the thermometer back up, wrote down the temperature, and then repeated with the rope at the twenty-foot mark. He got a canning jar, pulled up the sleeve of his sweatshirt, and reached as far over the edge of the float as he could to get his water sample. He loved the sweet, tangy smell of the ocean.

From above, a low, growly voice startled him. "What're you doing?"

Bear popped up and dropped his canning jar in the water. "Nothing. Science." Hiram Wiley climbed down the ladder from the pier. Bear backed away, nearly stepping off the float and into the ocean. With surprising speed, the old man reached into the sea, grabbed the jar, and handed it to Bear. "Thanks." Bear took the glass jar from the giant hand and clutched it to his chest. "I'm just doing schoolwork."

"Need any help?" Hiram Wiley's steely gray eyes stared from an expressionless face.

"No. No." Bear bent to pick up his backpack without taking his eyes off the lobsterman. "No, thank you, sir," he said as he climbed up the wooden ladder to the pier. *Sir.* Why did he say *sir*? Bear picked up speed. "Gotta go." He didn't look back and he didn't care that the jars were clanking together in the backpack.

His next stop was the ferry pier. He should be safe there.

When Bear finished taking temperatures and labeling his water sample, the ferry was approaching. Olivia would be on that boat. He packed up his belongings and waited by the ramp to meet her. He had to tell her all about Hiram Wiley.

Three boys about his age were the first to get off the ferry. They all wore bright yellow foul-weather gear, even though it hadn't rained in days. One of them carried a case as they joked and shoved each other. Suddenly, the boy with the black case raced up and stood in front of Bear, blocking his view of the other passengers walking off the boat.

"Hey, are you that Bear kid? Olivia's friend?"

Bear hesitated. The boy looked tough. "Yes," he said slowly and stepped back. Olivia had told him how mean the other kids were to her.

"She wasn't in school today." The stranger pulled open the snaps on his bright yellow rain jacket. "She okay?"

"She went to school," Bear said. "She told me she was going." Bear's certainty faded. He remembered the hard kick to his shin at the supper table and the nod. Had she said anything when he'd asked her last night? "You're sure? She's not on the boat?" Bear stretched to try and look around the boy.

"We were all looking for her." The other two boys joined them.

Why were they looking for her? This didn't sound good. Maybe she hid on the ferry so they wouldn't find her. She could be waiting for them to leave so she could get off the boat. That's what he would do. He needed to distract them.

He started to walk up the hill, hoping they would follow so she could get off the boat without having to worry about these bullies. The two new guys looked even bigger and tougher than the first one.

"Why?" Bear's voice broke. He looked around for a familiar face in the flow of people walking up Wharf Street from the boat. How could it be that he did not see one person who could help him and Olivia? Frank Peabody walked by, but Bear recognized him too late and couldn't think of any way to get his attention.

"My grampa told me about how kids have been picking on her," one of the boys said.

Bear turned back to them. "Your grampa?"

The boy with the case spoke. "Hiram Wiley. He's my gramps."

Bear stopped in front of the Goofy Gull Gift Shop and faced the three boys. He looked at the grandson. He had the same steely gray eyes as the lobsterman. Bear was afraid of stone-faced, pipe-smoking, huge-handed Hiram Wiley, but his grandson did seem concerned about Olivia. Maybe Bear had been wrong.

"Hey!" They all turned toward the voice. It was Olivia. "I was headed to your house," she said to Bear.

"You skipped school!" Bear said.

"You skipped school?" the three boys repeated.

"No. Did not. My dad needed help. He can't get around until your grampa puts a motor on his chair," Olivia said to the boy with the case. "He sprained his wrist."

They all nodded. The whole island knew that.

"Do you guys know each other?" Olivia asked.

"Not really," Bear said. He was feeling embarrassed for assuming they were bullies.

"Lenny." Hiram's grandson waved his case as a greeting. "I play the violin."

"He's good," everyone else said.

"Miguel." The second boy started bouncing a soccer ball on his right foot.

"I'm Asa," the third boy said as he smiled. "That was awesome how you two caught that poacher." He was referring to Bear's September visit to the island.

"We wanted to talk to you," Lenny said to Olivia.

"Looked for you all day. Cafeteria, library, your locker," Miguel said.

"Every deck on the ferry," Asa added.

"Couldn't find you, so we talked to your friend, Ubah."

"What?" Olivia looked genuinely surprised.

"We're going to eat lunch with all of you. Sit at your table. If that's okay. That should stop the other kids." He didn't say *from picking on you*, but they all knew what Lenny meant. Before Olivia could speak, he continued, "My grampa and I can drive over to your house and get your dad hooked up with the motor. Is he home?" Lenny must have realized that with a sprained wrist and without Olivia, Victor had to be at home. "Never mind. Yeah. We'll go right over."

"My turn to pull the traps," Asa said.

"I'll go with you," Miguel said. The two boys ran toward Mooney's Market, tossing the soccer ball between them.

Lenny headed off to find his grandfather at the fish house. "Bye," he shouted back to Bear and Olivia.

Olivia stood on the corner, looking back and forth between the boys heading off in opposite directions. "Wow. That was nice." She sat down on the curb and Bear joined her.

"Now you can go to school. No one will pick on you with those guys around."

"That's only part of the problem."

Bear waited, knowing Olivia would speak when she was ready.

"The coach is still a jerk," she said, and then, after another long pause, she continued. "I really did kind of skip school today. We could have come up with another plan for Dad, but I couldn't do my English homework."

"You're afraid of English?"

Olivia punched him in the shoulder. Two months earlier he would have winced, but now he just laughed and stood up. "Come on."

She hesitated.

"Come on. I know who can help you." Bear grabbed her wrist and pulled her toward the road. He was surprised when she let him.

When they arrived at Maple Street, he walked past his grandmother's house and into Mrs. Frost's living room without knocking. The Professor and Mrs. Frost were bent over a puzzle.

"Come in. Come in," Mrs. Frost said, although they were already in. "Sorry"—she didn't look up—"we're rushing to finish this so I can get my sewing machine set up." She tapped the table by way of explanation.

"How may we assist you?" the Professor asked, but he didn't look away from the puzzle pieces either.

Olivia shrugged.

Bear took a step toward them and spoke to the Professor. "Olivia needs your help."

"I do?"

"You do."

Now they had the adults' attention. Bear continued, "She's afraid of English." He hopped away from her before she could punch his shoulder again. He hoped she would be mad enough to explain what was really bothering her.

"Am not." She put her hands on her hips. Everyone waited patiently. "I can read." She tugged at her hair. "There's nothing wrong with my writing."

"Of course not, dear," Mrs. Frost said.

Olivia ducked her head and spoke quietly. "But I can't write about reading." She exhaled loudly as her shoulders drooped. "Themes, points of view, figurative and connotative text, compare and contrast, blah, blah, BLAH." The last *blah* was said with force. "What's the point? To ruin a good story?"

The Professor turned to her with a large grin on his face. "Maybe."

Olivia relaxed and almost smiled.

"I would like to place a wager with you," the Professor said. "We work together on these thorny literary assignments. After several sessions if you feel that they *ruin a good story,* as you say, you win. If this increases your appreciation of the literary work, then you win too." He held his hand out to Olivia. "Deal?"

Now she was smiling as she stepped toward him with her hand outstretched. "Deal!"

Well, that was easy, Bear thought.

"Now, perhaps you can help me, Olivia. Do you happen to have a half-slip I could borrow? Not too lacy. Preferably white."

Olivia stepped back and looked at Bear. "What?"

"Don't worry, dear," Mrs. Frost said to Olivia before turning back to the Professor. "I found one. I haven't worn it in years. The elastic has let loose but—"

"Marvelous." The Professor clapped his hands together with delight.

Olivia grabbed Bear's arm and pulled him toward the front door. "We gotta go."

"Return in an hour and we'll peruse your homework," the Professor said.

She nodded. As soon as they were out the door, Olivia turned to Bear. "What was that about? Why does he want Mrs. Frost's old clothes? She's half his size. Weird."

"It must be for Halloween," Bear said. "Maybe he's going to dress up as a woman."

They both laughed at the idea of the very tall Professor wearing the bird-sized Mrs. Frost's clothing.

"If I have to do my homework with him, how will we have time to catch whoever's keeping illegal lobsters?"

"And build our pumpkin pyramid?"

"And make our costumes?"

"And I need help with my ocean samples and temperatures."

"You should ask Hiram Wiley. He's practically an oceanographer."

Why did everyone keep telling him to talk to Hiram Wiley?

12

Tuesday morning as Bear lay in bed, he decided to simplify his science project. If he gathered samples only off the three piers, he could do all his schoolwork today and have more time to get ready for Halloween. Who would know? Who would care? He scratched between Honey's ears as he thought.

He would know. He would care. The more he thought about it, the more he wondered if the water in the open ocean was different than water in the more protected bay. But if he stopped thinking about it... That would work. Then even he wouldn't care. He was brilliant.

Honey appeared to agree as she darted around his legs with her tail thumping against everything in the room.

"You want to have fun?"

She jumped up, putting her paws on Bear's chest and licking his face before he fell back on the bed, laughing. Half her body landed in his lap. "We can't go anywhere if you don't get off of me."

Honey immediately sat back on the floor, doing her best imitation of a well-behaved dog.

"I think I can get Gramma to let you come with me today, but you have to stay out of trouble." The golden retriever was another good reason to stay away from the slippery rocks and rough surf on the backshore.

His grandmother was easier to persuade than he had expected. "She can go if you promise not to let her dig and roll on the beach. It took forever to get her cleaned and brushed yesterday."

"Promise!" Bear said, but he knew it was never that simple with Honey the Wonder Dog.

Once outside, Bear found the Professor in the middle of the dirt road, balancing on his crutches.

"Are you going to see Hiram?" the Professor asked, without waiting for an answer. "Thought I'd ambulate. Medical professionals are dictating more exercise if I'm ever to graduate from crutches to a cane. I'll join you."

"But I'm not—" Bear didn't know what to say. "I was going to—" He couldn't go to the backshore with Honey. He could go to the Yacht Club first, but the fish house was on the way and it sounded like the Professor needed exercise and wanted company. "Okay."

It felt like it took a week, but they finally made it to the bottom of the hill. Alberta Goodhue was on the bed and breakfast's steps wearing a tiny apron covered with ghosts and witches. It seemed out of place with her Mrs. Claus face, but Halloween was in four days. She was holding a broom and talking to her son.

"Morning, Bear," she called out in her lilting, friendly voice. "Your dog looks like she's had a bath and some brushing."

"Who are these people?" the Professor whispered.

"Alberta Goodhue, the lobster lady, and her son Wayne," Bear murmured. Clearly, the Professor hadn't been getting out of the house very much since his accident.

Wayne extended a hand to help the Professor on the steps, and Bear noticed a gold watch on his wrist. Seemed unusual. The last time Bear had seen him he wore a shirt that was two sizes too small and missing a button. Bear glanced down to check for the shirt gap and tuft of belly hair. He was relieved to see everything was covered today.

"The name's Wayne. This is my mom, Alberta," he said as he shook the Professor's hand.

"Malcolm, Malcolm Yeats. It's a pleasure to meet you."

Alberta Goodhue was staring at the watch on her son's wrist. "Shouldn't be wearing that…" Her voice was quiet but sliced through the two men's introductions. After a pause, her smile and lilting voice returned. "Don't wanna damage it, dear. Give it to me. I'll keep it safe." She patted the small pocket on the front of her Halloween apron.

"No." Wayne sounded mad. He wrapped his right hand around the watch protectively.

The Professor politely changed the subject. "By chance, have either of you observed Hiram Wiley this morning?"

"You throw around a lotta big words," Alberta Goodhue said with a snort.

Her son blurted, "Mom! Knock it off," before turning to the Professor and mumbling, "Sorry."

"It's true." She looked back and forth between Bear and her son, saying, "You heard him." She jerked her head toward the Professor.

"He's a really smart professor," Bear said as Honey made a low growling sound in the back of her throat.

The Professor gently tugged on Bear's shoulder and spoke to Alberta Goodhue through a forced smile. "I'm delighted to mention that you speak precisely as I would expect." He turned to Bear, and the forced smile slid from his face. "We should leave now."

As they walked away, Bear said, "That was embarrassing."

The Professor stopped abruptly and turned to Bear. "For whom? For me?"

"No. Of course not. For her. Mrs. Goodhue."

"Aaah. I see." The Professor shook his head. "I'm afraid, Mr. Bear, that she is beneath embarrassment."

Bear didn't understand, so he switched topics. "Hey, are you going to be a woman for Halloween?"

The Professor laid a hand on Bear's shoulder and chuckled. "Now that would be embarrassing. I choose to believe I'm more creative than that tired old trope. You can decide if I'm correct when you see me on Halloween."

Why would he want a woman's slip if he wasn't dressing up as a woman? "I should get going. I can look for Hiram later," Bear said, but he had no intention of seeking out the craggy old lobsterman.

"I will attempt to summit Wharf Street before lunch time." The Professor frowned at the steep hill. His eyes drooped and his voice was dull.

Maybe he's tired from the walk. Everybody said crutches were hard and the Professor was so tall there was a lot of him to haul around. Bear watched his friend slowly move up the hill, six crutch steps, rest, six crutch steps, rest.

"Well, Honey, let's go to the club and get away from those people." He looked back over his shoulder. Alberta Goodhue and her son were obviously arguing. That woman is nothing like Mrs. Claus, Bear thought. "We can get our data and samples from these piers later." Honey leaned against his leg and swept the street with her tail.

13

As they walked to the Yacht Club, Bear reviewed everything that had happened that morning: Wayne's shiny gold watch, the change in Mrs. Goodhue's behavior. Were she and her son fighting? Something was going on, but what? Who could he trust? What if Alberta Goodhue was not the sweet old woman he had thought she was? She'd made fun of the Professor. Nobody did that. And Olivia didn't seem to like her.

Deep in his thoughts, Bear was halfway down the Yacht Club pier, trailed by Honey, when he heard the voice. "Whatcha doing, boy?"

How had he missed that warm pipe tobacco smell? He smelled it now. Hiram Wiley sat below Bear in a dory with two oars and a small outboard motor at his feet. The sun bounced off his bald head, which was shiny with sweat.

Bear had tried so hard to avoid talking to this gruff man. Instead, he had stumbled into a smoky trap.

Hiram wiped his head with an old dish cloth before putting on his frayed baseball cap. He removed the pipe from his mouth and repeated, "Whatcha doing?"

At least Honey wasn't growling at Hiram. No, her tail was swishing on the worn pier boards and her head was cocked to the side as if she had a question or two of her own for the old lobsterman. Maybe Bear should trust Honey's judgment.

Bear kicked one foot with the other before beginning slowly. "Schoolwork."

"Speak up, boy. Bear."

Bear had forgotten about Hiram's hearing. Should he ask all his questions? Hiram was sitting back in the small boat, waiting. "Schoolwork," Bear said loudly. "I have to check the temperature, salinity, and density of the water at different places."

The old man nodded his head. "Trying to find the pycnocline?"

"Yeah. Maybe?" Bear didn't know. He'd never heard of a pick-na-cline. "It's about layers in the ocean and the density of each layer."

"I was joking." Hiram didn't look like he was joking. "Not enough rope in that backpack."

Bear realized the old man's face was stern, but it wasn't mean or mocking. All of the questions that had been

117

building from the day before burst from him: Are there differences between the eastward and westward facing sides of the island? Could he, should he, gather data in tide pools? How could he get deep-water temperatures when there wasn't a pier or a float? Did he need to do his work when it was high tide? Low tide? Mid-tide? Bear sat down on the pier. Honey lay beside him and plopped her head in Bear's lap. They both waited for Hiram to tell them what to do. The old man puffed on his pipe and looked at Bear.

Then he responded with a few questions of his own. "What're your measuring instruments?"

Bear unpacked his backpack and held up the thermometer and hydrometer.

"You have a vertical water sampler in that bag?"

Bear didn't know what that was, but he peered into his backpack before shaking his head *no*.

"Tide chart?"

Bear pretended to search again before shaking his head.

"What about a life preserver?"

Bear cocked his head and looked at the lobsterman. "What?"

"Gonna look in that bag of yours?" The corners of Hiram's mouth began a slow curve upward as he watched Bear.

"No, I'm pretty sure there isn't one in there." He ducked his head and stroked Honey's silky ears.

Hiram stepped out of the dory onto the float. "If you'd like, I could help. I happen to be interested in oceanography too."

"Really?" Bear was relieved, but then he was worried. This was his number one suspect for the lobster crimes.

"I need to fetch that vertical water sampler and some life preservers, and then we can go out and get your data."

"Go out?"

"In the dory."

Bear peered down at the little battered rowboat. "In that? In the ocean?"

"This here's my grandson's dory. Don't imagine he'll mind if we borrow it. They row, but I'm too old for that foolishness. We'll use the engine." He gestured toward the small outboard motor leaning against the rowboat's seat, and then he climbed up the ladder to the pier. He walked away, leaving Bear on the pier, worrying about what was going to happen next.

Within minutes, Hiram returned with an orange plastic crate, two life preservers and some equipment. He easily carried the armload down the ladder and stepped into the tiny wooden boat. The dory rocked in response to Hiram's movements but he didn't seem to notice. "You coming?" he asked Bear and flipped over the crate and sat on it.

Bear looked back and forth between Honey and Hiram. How could Honey get down the ladder?

Hiram attached the motor to the stern of the boat. Then he climbed up the ladder, bent over, draped Honey over his shoulders, and stood up. Honey seemed content with her front legs and head on one side of Hiram's well-groomed beard and her hind legs and tail on the other. Bear was not as trusting. What was Hiram doing?

"Gotta get her down." Hiram answered the unspoken question. He easily made his way down the ladder with Honey hanging around his neck like a scarf.

The weight of the lobsterman and golden retriever caused the dory to jerk side to side when Hiram stepped into the boat. Bear watched from the pier, hoping they wouldn't tip into the cold water.

"Come on down." Hiram gestured to the ladder. He swayed with the motion of the boat. "Get her situated." Hiram nodded toward Honey, who was walking in circles.

Bear climbed down, then tried to step into the middle of the boat, but Honey was in the way. The dory tipped toward the float. Bear grabbed Honey's neck.

"Sit," Hiram said sternly.

Honey and Bear dropped to the floor of the boat. The boat stopped rocking and Hiram turned to look at them. He grinned and said to Bear, "You can sit on the bench. Unless you're comfortable in that puddle."

Bear pulled himself up, trying to keep all his weight centered so the boat would stay steady. He exhaled so forcefully his lips flapped against his teeth. The back of his pants was soaking wet. What had he gotten into? It had started with a few questions. Now he was headed out to sea with a man he didn't know, in a boat that should be named the *Leaky Bucket*. If he'd learned anything today, it was to trust Honey's instincts—and she did not look comfortable with their situation. She panted as her head jerked side to side.

"Jerky?" Hiram asked as he started up the motor.

Bear looked up and saw Hiram extending a hunk of shriveled meat toward him. It was disgusting. He scrunched his face and shook his head.

"For the dog. You have your own snacks."

Bear accepted the leathery beef and offered it to the golden retriever. "She likes it." Bear sounded as surprised as he felt.

"Most dogs do." Hiram handed a life jacket to Bear. "This is for you."

When their life jackets were on, they motored toward the southerly tip of the island, Bear pulled up his sweatshirt hood and tightened the string under his chin. He was wet and cold, but he enjoyed seeing the island and the ocean from their low position in the water—so low they were barely half a step up from swimming. That realization caused a jolt of anxiety. Honey snored quietly on his feet. That was reassuring.

"Thought we'd go to the shore near the beaver pond. You know the spot?" Hiram said.

Bear knew exactly where he meant. That's where the starfish pools were. "I fell in there yesterday trying to go out on the rocks," he hollered, so Hiram could hear him.

"'Magine," Hiram said, and pulled on his pipe. "This will be safer." They cruised along in silence for a while before Hiram spoke again. "Hope Olivia knows it's nothing new for island kids to be picked on at the mainland schools."

Bear looked at him blankly.

"Always been that way. For me. My kids. Now my grand-kids. We have our way of doing things and they have theirs. But kids can be cruel. Heck, so can grown-ups. It's not personal. They see her as being different. Because of how she dresses. The way she talks. Just like her friend whose dad is an engineer."

A couple months earlier, Bear had seen Olivia as different too. An hour earlier, he'd felt the same way about Hiram Wiley. Maybe that was the same thing. Bear nodded his head. He understood exactly what the old lobsterman was talking about. Hiram settled into his usual silence.

Bear was curious. "Your grandson, Lenny, he's a lobsterman too?"

Hiram nodded. "And a violinist. You can be both, but it's not very common."

"Does he work on your boat with you?"

"No. No. I won't let him. The sternman uses the winch." He held up his hand with the missing knuckles. "It'd be hard to play the violin with fingers like these. He and his buddies haul their traps by hand. It's hard work but safer. They stay close to shore and you don't have to worry about fingers getting snagged in the machinery."

It must have been Lenny and his friends that he and Olivia saw in the dinghy near Porcupine Island. No one would know if they were keeping oversized or undersized lobsters. They worked alone. When he looked up at Hiram's silhouette, he felt guilty for thinking his grandson might be breaking the state's conservation laws.

"Everyone told me I should ask you for help."

"I know."

Of course. Someone had told Hiram about Bear's school project. It was hard to keep a secret on an island.

At their first stop, the little boat bobbed gently in the calm waters near the rocks that protected the starfish pools. Hiram attached a thermometer to the vertical water sampler and dropped it into the water. Instead of scooping water from the surface, the sampler wouldn't let any water in until it was at the depth Bear wanted. When he pulled the sample into the boat, he asked Bear, "Are you doing pH testing?"

"I'll do that later. My teacher gave me these strips I dip in—" He stopped talking when he saw Hiram's expression.

Hiram was shaking his head. "Not accurate enough. Use this." He handed Bear a plastic gadget barely bigger than a candy bar. "It's already warmed up."

Bear handed it back. "I don't know how—"

"I'll show you." Hiram took the meter and the water sample. "Those test strips are only good for measuring whole units. We won't find any differences that great around the island. This," he said, holding up the meter, "is accurate to one-hundredth of a unit."

While Hiram rinsed the tip of the meter in a special solution, Bear admired the backshore of Oxbow Island. Everything looked different from the water. Wilder. The giant rocks that circled and protected the island from the rough surf were black and shiny from the ocean spray. In the first layers of soil behind the rocks were hearty rugosa roses gripping the sandy soil. Just beyond the roses was Atlantic Avenue, the only road around the island. Bear couldn't see it and the summer homes seemed shrunken from his water view.

"Look!" Bear pointed at two horses and their riders on the backshore.

Hiram looked toward shore and nodded. Bear examined the old man. He didn't look like someone who would break the law. But could you tell by looking at someone?

In less than two hours they circled the island, collecting data at Seal Rock and Mussel Beach. Bear grew comfortable using all of Hiram's equipment. He felt like a scientist by the time Hiram tied the dory to the float at Lobstermen's Pier.

"That was mid-tide. We can go one day at high tide and another at low tide if you want to compare."

"Sure. That would be great." The thought of a few hours in a small boat on the ocean with Hiram Wiley no longer scared Bear. But he still wasn't ready to remove the old man from his suspect list. Bear glanced at the ladder on the side of the pier and then back at Honey. "How?" he began, wondering whether Hiram would carry her up the ladder. He looked to the lobsterman for a plan.

"You take the equipment in your backpack. Scramble on up and head to the beach. I'll run the boat aground and she can hop out," Hiram said.

This seemed like an excellent plan until the boat neared the shore where Bear was waiting. Honey dove into the water before Hiram could land, swam to Bear, and then rolled in the sand over and over. She resisted Bear's attempts to stop her and get her to stand. "Honey, no. Honey, stop." He had promised his grandmother this wouldn't happen. Hiram was chuckling at the sight of the happy dog. "Gramma's going to kill me." Bear snapped the leash on her collar and tugged with all his might to keep her from going back to the lobster graveyard. "We have to get you home and cleaned up before anybody notices."

Tugging, urging, scolding, Bear dragged Honey away from the beach. They were almost to Water Street when he heard the lilting sing-songy voice.

"Oh, goodness, that's a dirty, dirty dog you have there." Alberta Goodhue laughed.

Bear kept tugging on Honey's leash, but she planted her hind quarters on the street and her tail was rigid behind her.

"This here's my gentleman friend." Alberta Goodhue gestured toward a man in a plaid shirt.

Bear hadn't even noticed him slouching against the fish house.

"Sorry 'bout what happened earlier," Alberta Goodhue said.

"That's okay," Bear said, even though it wasn't. Why had she been rude to the Professor? Bear tugged on Honey's leash again, but the dog was glaring at Alberta Goodhue.

"I don't know what's wrong with Wayne."

"Wayne?" What was she talking about? She was the one who had been rude to the Professor.

"My son. He's such a momma's boy. I think he's just jealous that I have a special friend." She dipped her head toward the fish house, but the unfamiliar man was gone.

What was she talking about? Honey gave the slightest growl deep in her throat. "I have to go," Bear said as he tried to pull Honey from her spot in the road.

"Bear! Honey!" Bear heard Victor calling from behind them. That was all it took to move Honey. She jumped and ran to her friend. With a slight whirring sound, Victor drove in a few tight circles.

"Your wheelchair is motorized! Ni-i-ice! Hiram did that?"

Victor's grin nearly swallowed his face as he nodded.

"I think I was wrong about him," Bear said, more to himself than to Victor.

"What have you done to Honey the Wonder Dog?" Victor laughed as she put her sandy wet paws in his lap and licked his face. He tried to avoid her smelly, dirty, wet belly, but it was hopeless. His shirt and pants were covered with sand when she got off his lap.

"I have to get her home and clean before Gramma sees her. I promised—"

"I'm on my way to your grandmother's house to ask for a little help on a project. I can distract her while you shampooch."

"Shampooch?"

"Did Honey do the doggie paddle?" Victor always laughed at his own jokes. "You two stay here. Give me five minutes to get your grandmother out of the house and over to Mrs. Frost's. Then you can try to take the beach out of the dog."

With his new motor humming, Victor went up the hill twice as fast as the Professor had that morning. He was gone before Bear could ask why he needed his grandmother's help.

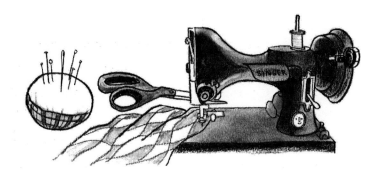

14

Wednesday morning, Bear woke to a silent house. Even Honey wasn't staring down at him, begging him to get out of bed. Where was everyone? He wandered downstairs and plopped on the couch. He couldn't see anyone on Maple Street or Mrs. Frost's front porch. Were they all getting ready for Halloween? The day before he had been able to scrub the sand off Honey and even use his grandmother's blow dryer to dry the dog without anyone noticing. What was everyone working on? It was hours before he was going to meet Hiram Wiley at the Lobstermen's Pier. Hiram was out in his lobster boat checking his traps. After that, he was taking Bear out to gather data at low tide.

Bear wandered into the kitchen for breakfast and found a box of cereal and a note from his grandmother. She had a "little project" and was at Mrs. Frost's with her sewing machine. He was NOT to come over. She also thanked him for giving Honey such a thorough bath. She had noticed. And Honey would be staying at Mrs. Frost's. That was probably best, after what happened yesterday. Bear pressed his face against the living room window, hoping he'd be able to see into Mrs. Frost's house. When that didn't work, he went into the front yard and began moving pumpkins around. He circled the pumpkins and the pyramid structure while keeping an eye on Mrs. Frost's. He tried not to stare in case anyone was watching him. He could see his grandmother and Mrs. Frost side by side at their sewing machines inside the windows.

With hours left before he had to meet Hiram, he might as well try to stack the pumpkins. The first row was easy. The second row was a little harder. Each pumpkin on the bottom had to be shifted so its stem fit between the pumpkins balanced on top of it. The third row was impossible. Bear put five in place, stepped back, and one after another they rolled, bounced, and crashed on the lawn. It was only a matter of time before one broke open. With only four extra pumpkins, he had to be careful.

"Good morning, Bear. Looks like that's coming along." Victor had snuck up on him again. "Olivia wishes she could help more. Between school, cross-country, and studying with the Professor, she doesn't have a spare minute."

"I could use her help." Bear sat down on a pumpkin.

"I'd offer, but I have an important appointment." He motored off to Mrs. Frost's house, leaving Bear alone again.

Bear stared at Victor's back as he rolled up the ramp. What was Victor doing? The Professor had to be in there too. Did they both sew? Anything was possible.

Bear looked back at the pyramid. He circled the plywood and metal structure again. He needed help. But everyone on the island was busy with their own projects. They didn't have time for him. What was the point? He might as well do his math homework for the week. He retreated into the house and his list of school assignments until it was time to meet Hiram Wiley.

After two hours of math problems with decimals, Bear was eager to be outside on the ocean. He ran down to the Lobstermen's Pier and was surprised to see Hiram scrubbing the side of his lobster boat with a giant sponge.

"Just got in," Hiram said as Bear stepped into the boat. "I'll wipe down this gunwale and then we can head out."

Bear could see and smell the seaweed and bait that had been dragged across the side of the boat with each trap Hiram had hauled that morning. Several seagulls circled above, squawking and calling for bait. Bear looked around the boat while Hiram put the lid on the barrel of salted herring he used in his bait bags. There were freshly caught lobsters in a large plastic barrel filled with water. The lobsters had thick rubber bands around their claws to keep them from latching on to a finger or another lobster. They all appeared to be of legal size.

Hiram started the engine. It was a lot louder than the little outboard motor they had relied on the day before. Bear would really have to yell if he wanted Hiram to hear him today. The lobster boat edged away from the pier and headed toward Mussel Beach.

"Hey, Hi, why do you know so much about oceanography?" Bear hollered.

"I'm a lobsterman."

Bear looked back blankly. That sounded like the opposite of an explanation.

"I want to put my traps where the lobsters are. Lobsters are like Goldilocks. They don't like the water too hot or too cold. They don't like the water too salty or not salty enough. They like it *just right*. I've been gathering samples for years." He stroked his silver beard before adding, "Plus I'm just plain curious."

"Me too."

The old man and the boy looked at each other and nodded. "The ocean's been warming since I was a boy. The lobsters are moving north and farther out. I have fifty years of temperatures."

"Wow!" Bear's little experiment seemed silly compared to Hiram's lifetime of gathering data.

"They like the water salty. I don't put my traps where there's a lot of freshwater run-off, like the mouth of a river. You get two days of heavy rain, the salinity drops and the lobsters will find a new home."

"Really? They move?"

Hiram nodded and looked toward the open ocean. "The pH is dropping. Water's getting more acidic. That's bad for all shellfish, not just lobsters. Makes it hard for them to build a strong shell."

The lobster boat cruised along, bouncing off the wakes of other boats. Bear grabbed a handrail to steady himself as he thought about what Hiram had said. Bear finally understood why everyone had told him to ask Hiram for help.

"Hey, Hi."

Hiram turned toward Bear and raised his bushy eyebrows in a questioning gesture.

Bear remembered he had to holler. "Why is it against the law to keep all the lobsters you catch? Big or little?" he asked without thinking.

"It's good for us lobstermen. And it's better for the lobsters."

Obviously, it was good for the lobsters that were thrown back in the ocean, but how could that be good for the lobstermen and women? Bear waited for an explanation.

"I want there to be lobsters for my grandchildren and their grandchildren."

Bear nodded.

"If I get a berried lobster in my pot—"

"What?" Bear blurted. He had seen plenty of buried lobster under the Lobstermen's Pier.

Hiram smiled. "Female lobster with eggs. In my trap. They'll have thousands of them on their bellies at the base of their tails. The eggs look like berries." Hiram paused and checked to see if Bear understood.

Berried, not *buried*. Bear nodded his head.

"I cut a V in her tail and throw her back. I want her to reproduce so there are lots more lobsters. That's better for everyone than me getting one more lobster that day. Anyone else catches her, even after the eggs are gone, they'll see that V in her tail and throw her back too. It's good for all of us. Guarantees there will still be lobsters out here in the future." Hiram gestured toward Casco Bay. "Same with the little lobsters. We want them to grow big enough to reproduce at least once."

That made sense. "But what about the really big ones?" Bear asked.

"I like to think it's because they survived so long, they've earned the right to live out the rest of their lives in peace. Like me. Did you know they can live fifty to a hundred years?"

Bear's eyes widened. One hundred years. That was even older than Mrs. Frost.

"Older they get, the more fertile they are, and I suppose that's the reason behind the law." He leaned back and smoke rose from the end of his pipe.

The boat slowed down and the engine quieted. "They call this Mussel Beach because you used to be able to come to these rocks and gather fresh mussels for your dinner. You'd find them as big as my thumb."

Bear stared at Hiram's huge thumb.

"For the last ten years or more you only see the little ones. The size of my fingernail." Hiram held up his pinky finger, the size of a plump breakfast sausage. "We don't want that happening to lobsters. Now most of the mussels you get are farmed."

"Farmed?"

"They grow them on ropes."

Bear nodded, pretending to understand. After listening to Hiram talk about lobsters, it didn't make sense that he could be responsible for the lobster graveyard Honey had dug up. He was too concerned with protecting lobstering. Did that mean his son and grandson felt the same way?

Bear had to ask one more question. "Hey, Hi. Do you call the police or the harbor master if you see someone breaking the law on the ocean?"

Hiram's head snapped up. "You could." He tugged on his beard and looked at Bear. "John and Betty would call the Marine Patrol. They're in charge out here. Why?" He looked intently at Bear. There was no trace of a smile on the craggy face. "Who do you want to turn in?"

Bear had said too much. "No. No one. Just curious. That's all." He tried to make a joke. "I didn't think Officer Calvin would swim out here to arrest someone." Bear laughed nervously.

Hiram didn't. For the next hour he barely spoke. There was the occasional syllable about the water temperature, salinity, or pH levels. But nothing that resembled a sentence. The seagulls were better company than Hiram Wiley lost in his thoughts. Bear was relieved when he finally saw Lobstermen's Pier.

"See you here tomorrow. Eight o'clock sharp." He didn't look at Bear when he spoke.

"Thanks." Bear hopped off the boat with his backpack clutched in his hand. The lobster boat pulled away from the float and Bear plopped onto the wooden boards to think about their conversation. What did Hiram's silence mean? Something had changed when Bear asked about calling the police.

15

As Bear sat on the float thinking, he noticed a wooden crate bobbing in the water by his feet. He lay on his stomach and peered inside the wet wooden box. It was hard to see into the dark water. Something rose to the surface. Bear pulled back before realizing the box was an underwater cage. Whatever was inside couldn't get out. He hung his head over the edge of the float to get a closer look. There were live lobsters, lots of them, in the box, floating in the seawater.

Every day he had more questions than the day before. As he walked toward the beach, he looked down through the boards of the pier to see if the lobster graveyard had been disturbed. It seemed untouched since he and Honey had reburied her treasure trove. It was Wednesday and they weren't any closer to figuring out who was responsible for all those illegal lobster shells. He didn't have a lot of time left on the island.

When he looked up, he saw Alberta Goodhue hauling two buckets up the steps to the bed and breakfast. She was bent over by the weight. Buckets of water for mopping floors? Why would she be carrying them into the Seabreeze? It was weird. What was she doing? He shook his head. He needed to stay focused.

With renewed energy, Bear walked to the ferry dock to gather data. As he pulled up the vertical water sampler, he saw the car ferry crossing the bay. By the time he was packing up his notebook and tools, people were getting off the ferry. Frank Peabody was in a group of islanders walking up the ramp. Maybe he knew what Alberta Goodhue had in those buckets. Why not ask? Bear's curiosity could not be ignored.

He dashed over to meet Frank at the top of the ramp. "Hi." He struggled to sound casual. "I noticed Alberta Goodhue carrying some really…heavy…buckets…" As the words trickled from his mouth, Bear heard how ridiculous he sounded.

Frank Peabody's head dipped a little more to the side with each new word.

"I wondered—"

"What?" Frank asked.

Bear examined the innkeeper's face and decided to stop before he made a total fool of himself. "Nothing." He cleared his throat. "They looked really heavy."

Frank appeared puzzled.

"I thought—" Bear searched every corner of his brain for words that could end the conversation. "I thought I should've offered to help. That's all."

Frank Peabody smiled and patted him on the shoulder. "That's very considerate of you."

Bear exhaled loudly as Frank walked away, up the hill. He really needed to improve his interrogation skills. His questions led to silence and confusion rather than answers. At least Bear's fake concern had impressed the innkeeper. The last stop of the day would be the Yacht Club. No one would be there. What a relief. Then he could go back to his grandmother's and stack some pumpkins.

The moment Bear's foot touched the first wooden plank of the Yacht Club pier, he noticed movement below him on the water. He pulled his foot back. Someone was in one of the dories. Hiram? Bear sniffed the air for the scent of pipe smoke and took two steps backwards. He could wait somewhere, on the tennis courts, maybe, until the person left.

"Hey," a voice called out. It wasn't the low, gruff sound of Hiram Wiley.

Bear walked slowly toward the voice, looking down at the finger float. Who had called out? A boy was seated in the dory Bear and Hiram had used the day before. It was Lenny. Bear hadn't recognized him without his violin case.

"Hi." Bear raised his hand a few inches in a half-hearted attempt to wave. Then he noticed a wooden crate in the water. It was just like the one he'd seen at the Lobstermen's Pier. "What's that?" Bear pointed at the wooden box floating just below the water's surface.

"Lobster car." Lenny sounded friendly. "We keep the lobsters in there until we sell them." He didn't seem annoyed by Bear's questions.

All the lobstermen must do that, Bear thought. "You heading over to Porcupine Island?"

"No, that's too far to row. Although Grampa left this sweet motor in here for me to use today. All our traps are along the shore. Hard enough to pull them by hand without having to row across the shipping channel too." He gestured toward Oxbow Island's coastline. "Safer here. I don't like to take this little peapod out where the big boats are."

But somebody did. Bear and Olivia had seen him. "There are some traps over there," Bear said.

"Yup. Some old guy fishes those pots. I've seen him from the ferry." Lenny didn't stop working. He continued loading and organizing his supplies in the dory. "He's not from around here. I think he's selling them in town. Today, I was getting off the school bus at the ferry terminal and I saw a guy on the street with a sign and a cooler. Bet it's the same guy and I bet he makes a lot more money than we do selling them to the co-op." He untied the dory, sat down, and pushed off from the float. "Gotta go pull some traps."

Who was the mystery man hauling traps around Porcupine Island? If he sold his lobsters in Portland and didn't live on the island, then he couldn't be responsible for the lobster graveyard. Lenny and his friends kept their lobsters in the ocean by the Yacht Club and sold them to the co-op in Portland. They were never near the Lobstermen's Pier either. Bear worked his way through his list of suspects. There was Wayne Goodhue. But he didn't look like a lobsterman and he wasn't on the island very often. It had to be one of the grown-up island lobstermen. Olivia had said there were six on the island. They needed their names and fishing schedules.

Bear wrote down his data in the notebook. When he looked up, he saw the ferry crossing Casco Bay again. Olivia should be on that boat. He had to catch her before she walked up the hill to meet with the Professor. As he ran, he made a list in his head. At the top of his list was Hiram Wiley, second was his son Fuzzy, and then there were four others. He had to show Olivia the lobster graveyard.

The first passengers were walking up the hill from the boat as he turned the corner at the Goofy Gull Gift Shop. He spotted her immediately. She was still in her running clothes from cross-country practice. Her head hung low, and she looked at her feet as she made her way up Wharf Street.

"Olivia," Bear shouted. "Over here."

She shook her head and made no move to join him on the sidewalk. "I have to see the Professor about my paper—"

"Come here," he hissed, and she reluctantly joined him. "This won't take long." He looked around before moving closer to the closed gift shop and whispering, "I need the names of all the lobstermen on the island."

"Okay—"

Before she could answer he continued, "It's not Lenny and his friends fishing around Porcupine Island. It's some old guy who sells the lobsters on the sidewalk in Portland."

"I just saw him. Over there." Olivia nodded toward Portland. "So?"

"So, we can rule him out and we can rule out Lenny, Miguel, and Asa as suspects."

"Obviously. What are you doing all day? I could have told you that three days ago."

"Well." Bear stopped to think. "It's hard. Everyone clams up when I ask the important questions."

"That's because they're the important questions." She didn't say *duh*, but Bear heard it in her voice.

"Yeah." Bear paused. "Hiram told me about cutting out a V in lobsters' tails if they are breeding females. No one's supposed to keep those lobsters. What if there are V-notched tails in the lobster graveyard?"

Olivia smiled. "Now you're thinking." Wharf and Water streets were empty again. All of the ferry passengers had headed home for the day. Still, she whispered. "We can't just walk over there. Someone could see us. Let's head down Water Street past the Lobstermen's Pier like we're just taking a walk. Then we can sneak down the hill on the other side, by the people graveyard."

As they approached the top of the steep path, Bear and Olivia paused in front of the modest tombstones.

"Two sisters and two brothers." Bear knelt before the Frost family headstones.

"I've known these were here my whole life," Olivia said. "I never thought about the people."

Bear rose. "How many more do you think—" He struggled to ask his questions about what or who might be in the ground beneath his feet. He backed up, lost in thought.

"Careful!" Olivia grabbed his arm before he stepped off the edge of the cliff. "Come on. Let's get out of here."

Getting down the steep hill was even harder than climbing it had been. When their feet slid out from under them, they grabbed on to whatever plant was nearby. Half the time it was a wild rose bush with sharp thorns that cut into their hands. Eventually they decided to just sit down and slide the rest of the way, landing at the bottom with a bounce.

The lobster graveyard seemed unchanged since the last time Bear and Honey had been there. Packed, smooth sand surrounded a large circle of disturbed sand where they had filled in the pit. No lobster shells were visible on the surface.

"This it?" Olivia asked.

Bear nodded his head, knelt down, and began to push away the sand. Olivia mirrored his movements on the opposite side.

Within a minute Bear was holding a lobster tail with a V cut from the end. "Check it out," he whispered. He set the tail beside him and continued. He held up a claw: "too big." And then another: "too small." He sat back on his heels and said, "Have you noticed there aren't any Goldilocks lobsters here?"

"What?"

Thinking of Hiram, he said, "Too big. Too little. Nothing here is *just right*. Goldilocks would not be happy."

Olivia smiled.

"This should be enough evidence." Bear picked up the tail and two claws. He walked over to Olivia's side of the graveyard to pick up her shells.

"No. We shouldn't take them. First, because people might see us walking with them. But more important, if we call the police—"

"Marine Patrol," Bear corrected.

"Really?" She stood up and brushed the sand off her knees. "When we report this, shouldn't the crime scene be exactly the way we found it?"

"The moment Honey found this, it was too late for that," Bear said. He stood thinking for a moment. Olivia was probably right. Besides, it wouldn't look good to have any of these illegal shells in their possession. He already had two giant claws in his closet. Bear quickly dug a hole and tossed the shells in. "Maybe you're right." He pushed sand over the shells with his foot. "But that means that we have nothing. You know that? And this could all be cleaned up in one night. Leaving us with a pit and no evidence."

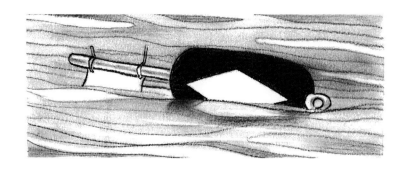

16

Thursday morning Bear had to hurry to meet Hiram at the Lobstermen's Pier. They were going out at eight o'clock to take their measurements at high tide. The more Bear thought about it, the sillier his research seemed. Hiram had decades of data and he said he'd graphed it all. Why didn't Bear just use that? Hiram's would look a lot more impressive than anything Bear could do in three days. He could ask Hiram. Then Bear would have more time to figure out who was keeping illegal lobsters, stack the pumpkins, and make his costume. He had almost forgotten about trick-or-treating, and Halloween was in two days.

As Bear walked down Wharf Street, he thought through different ways to ask his questions. He needed answers, not stony silence. He needed to be a detective. He needed to get information without revealing his suspicions. He needed to put his suspect at ease. Bear laughed out loud at the thought of the stone-faced Hiram Wiley at ease and chatting away.

"Hey, Hi." Bear waved as he ran down the dock. "You checking your traps this afternoon?" He needed to start his questioning like they were having a regular conversation.

"Nope." He pulled on his pipe. "Just check them every other day."

The sound of the motor starting replaced their voices. Bear paced behind Hiram, looking around for something, anything, to ask about.

"You okay, boy?" Hiram had turned to watch Bear.

Under the forceful gaze of Hiram Wiley, Bear blurted, "Do you know who has the traps around Porcupine Island?"

"Hadn't paid them any mind," Hiram said. "Saw the buoys over there but didn't think much about it." He turned the boat's wheel hard to the left. With those words they headed away from Oxbow Island, toward Portland.

What was Hiram doing? Bear began to worry. Every time he asked an important question everything went sideways.

Hiram slowed the boat as they approached Porcupine Island. He looked carefully at the buoys dotting the small island's coastline. "Never seen that pattern before."

"Pattern?"

"Every lobsterman, woman paints their buoys with a different color pattern. Each one is registered with the state.

Now you've got me curious. I'll find out who they belong to." Hiram turned and smiled at Bear before turning the boat's wheel and steering toward their backshore test sites.

Bear stood next to Hiram and looked out over the prow of the lobster boat. "Hey, Hi." When the old man didn't turn his head, Bear raised his voice and tried again. "You said you'd graphed years' worth of temperatures and salinity levels…"

Hiram nodded one time before turning to examine Bear's face. The only sound was the squawking of the seagulls begging to sample Hiram's smelly bait. He ignored them and spoke slowly. "When you have your study all written, we can discuss our findings. Yours and mine." The boat bumped up and down as they crossed another boat's wake. "Science is all about the process. No point in jumping to the conclusion. Mine or yours. Conclusions are meaningless unless you understand the process." He turned back to scan the open ocean as they rounded the northeastern edge of Oxbow Island.

He had known what Bear wanted before Bear had even asked. Hiram Wiley should be the detective, not Bear. But he was one of Bear's suspects, so that wouldn't work.

By the time they reached Seal Rock, they had relaxed into a comfortable silence. Hiram slowed the boat and the engine quieted to a low rumble. Bear was removing the vertical sampler and thermometer from his backpack when

Hiram tapped his shoulder. Bear looked where Hiram was pointing. Five seals were sunning themselves on the rock. The boat drifted toward them with each swell. The seals lifted their heads and watched the drifting boat.

Hiram pointed to the bait bucket. "You can throw them some."

Without hesitating, Bear grabbed hunks of dead, smelly herring and threw them as hard as he could toward the rock. The seals looked clumsy on land but moved faster than Bear expected. Within seconds they were sliding into the water and out of sight. For a moment Bear was disappointed, but then he saw five heads pop up beside the boat. Their faces reminded him of Honey begging to go out on a walk.

"One each," Hiram said as he handed more bait to Bear.

The seals popped up to catch the bait as it dropped from Bear's hands. Hiram handed him a towel to wipe the bait off his hands. "They can be rascals, but I enjoy watching them move," Hiram said. "I'm afraid if you drop that in now"—he gestured toward the vertical sampler—"they'll take a bite. Let's head over to the starfish pools. We can come back later for your measurements."

Bear leaned against the prow of the lobster boat and watched the gray, silky seals swim behind them for several minutes before they turned back toward Seal Rock.

"That was cool," he said as he joined Hiram at the ship's wheel.

The old man's gray eyes smiled back at him as he patted Bear's shoulder in agreement. Hiram was silent, but it didn't bother Bear. Some moments were suited to silence.

Bear made it home in time for lunch, but he was still not allowed at Mrs. Frost's. Alone at his grandmother's house, he ate a sandwich his grandmother had left for him and began to make a chart of the data he had collected. He could see a few trends. Water temperatures were slightly lower and the pH was slightly higher on the backshore. Based on what Hiram had told him, that was the best place to put lobster traps. Too bad it was so far for Lenny, Miguel, and Asa to row there. And even though his measurements hadn't been taken very far underwater, he could still see some differences in density between the surface and twenty feet below. Decimals were proving to be more helpful than he had ever imagined. He wrote up a conclusion, tucked his tidy chart away, and looked up at the clock. It was almost three-thirty. He could run down to the dock and see if Olivia was on this boat.

Out of habit he stopped and ducked behind a shrub when he reached the intersection of Wharf and Water streets. He looked toward Mooney's Market, down to the dock, and then toward the fish house. Two lobstermen stood talking beside the shack. Nothing unusual there. He glanced at the front of the bed and breakfast. Bent at the waist, arms dragging at her sides, Alberta Goodhue was again struggling to carry two white buckets into the Seabreeze. Bear knew better than to ask Frank Peabody about the buckets. She changed sheets, cleaned bathrooms, vacuumed, and baked cookies. None of those tasks required carrying heavy buckets up the front steps of the bed and breakfast.

When Alberta disappeared through the front doors, Bear raced down the hill to meet the ferry. He hoped Olivia was on this boat. Then he saw her, head held high, trotting toward him.

"You're in a good mood." Seeing Olivia happy made Bear realize how unhappy she had been.

"No cross-country practice." She jumped in the air to do a high-five that Bear completely missed. "Coach wants us rested up for tomorrow's meet. And all of the girls have agreed to wear the hats your grandmother bought. He'll have to let Ubah run with her hijab."

This time Bear jumped up for a high-five, but Olivia's feet remained firmly planted on the ground.

"What're you doing down here? Shouldn't you be measuring something?"

"There's something I want to check out. Okay? Maybe it's nothing. But it could be something."

"Just tell me."

Bear lowered his voice. He spoke in code in case anyone could hear him. "Two times I've seen Mrs. Claus carrying heavy packages. It's not Christmas. You know what I mean?"

Olivia shook her head.

He spoke more slowly. "We need to know what's in the packages."

"I have no idea what you're talking about, but let's do it."

Bear's mouth dropped open. Olivia must be in a really good mood. She never agreed to anything so easily. "We can't go in the front door. We might run into someone. I thought we could sneak around to the back. There's a lot of bushes we could hide—" Olivia was already walking away. "The B and B. We're going to the B and B," he hollered at her back.

She turned back and laughed. "Very smooth, Sherlock." When he caught up to her, she spoke quietly. "The kitchen's in the back. There's a door."

They ducked behind the tall shrubs next to the bed and breakfast, waiting, listening, looking. When they were sure no one was around, they crawled on their hands and knees beside the building. At the first window they both raised their heads and looked in. The kitchen was empty. The crawled to the second window and checked again before scurrying to the door. Olivia poked her head into the kitchen while Bear pressed his body flat against the wall. When she turned and gave him the thumbs up, they both crept quietly through the door.

Inside the silent kitchen they looked at each other. What now? They could hear footsteps above their heads and a hissing boiling sound coming from the stove in the corner. Bear turned toward the stove and saw a giant steaming pot. On the floor in front of the stove were two white buckets. He darted in that direction, eager to see what Alberta Goodhue had been carrying into the building.

His first step landed in a metal bucket filled with soapy water. He jerked his foot out and knocked over the bucket with a loud clanging noise. As he reached for the bucket, he could hear Olivia's panicked whisper: "Quiet." And then he knocked over a mop that had been leaning against the counter. Another crashing sound and the footsteps above his head were on the move. They had to get out, but Bear couldn't leave until he found out what Alberta Goodhue had in those buckets. Sliding across the wet floor, Bear glanced into the buckets and saw a live lobster with a V cut out of its tail on top of other thrashing lobsters. The footsteps clamored down the stairs. They were coming. Bear used the counter for balance as he surfed back across the wet floor. Olivia was frantically waving at him through the window. Bear looked at her and nearly tripped over the fallen mop. He grabbed the counter and hopped over the mop and metal bucket before a final push across the sudsy floor.

The footsteps were in the hallway. Someone was on the other side of the kitchen door. Bear slipped out the back door and dropped to his knees.

"Who made this mess in my kitchen?" It was Alberta Goodhue.

He scurried on his knees to the shrub by the road. Olivia was there. She grabbed his arm and pulled him out to the road just as he was trying to catch his breath.

"Run! Run!" she hissed before racing up Wharf Street.

In his whole life, Bear had never run so fast. He was gasping for breath and urging his legs up the steep hill. With each step he was farther behind Olivia. He listened for the sound of someone behind him. He knew Alberta Goodhue couldn't run up this hill, but he expected someone to grab him by the shirt and pull him back down the hill. He rubbed the back of his neck without breaking stride, checking to see if there was a hand there. He would hear footsteps or their breathing if someone were following him; still, he urged his feet to go faster.

When he reached his grandmother's house, where Olivia waited for him, Bear collapsed on the grass beside the pumpkin pile, gasping for air. After a minute of watching his chest heave up and down, he rose to his feet and bent over with his hands on his knees, afraid he might throw up.

"What did you see?"

Bear couldn't speak. He held up two fingers in the shape of a V.

Olivia's eyes widened.

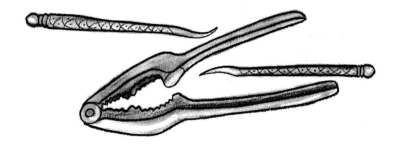

17

When he recovered, Bear told Olivia about the V-notched lobster. He was positive. A giant pot of water had been on the stovetop with steam escaping from beneath the lid. Bear had not seen what was inside, but he guessed it was filled with boiling lobsters. The white bucket on the floor was full to the brim with water, seaweed, and more lobsters. There was no mistaking it, the lobster on top had an obvious V cut out of its twitching tail. Olivia and Bear knew they were on the right track. Was Frank Peabody part of the scheme? Or was Alberta doing this without his knowledge? They needed help and quickly agreed that Hiram Wiley was the person to ask. They had to catch him the next morning before he went out lobstering.

Friday morning at five-thirty it was dark as a closet, and Honey lay snoring on the floor beside Bear's bed when the alarm jolted him up from his soft pillow. Why? What? He struggled to remember and to shut off the noise. He lay back on the pillow. He had told Olivia to sleep in because she had her cross-country meet and needed to rest up. He had agreed to go to the fish house alone, in the dark. He was having serious second and third thoughts about being so considerate. But he had to get moving if he was going to catch Hiram. He stepped over Honey, who didn't bother to lift her head or wag her tail.

She was still sound asleep when Bear was dressed, but she had to go with him. There was no way he was walking the dark, empty streets of Oxbow Island all alone. She always saw and heard things before he did and could warn him. He had to get her up quietly and sneak out of the house without waking his grandmother. Bear whispered, nudged, and tugged gently on her collar. When Honey realized he was serious about heading outside, she perked up—but that meant her tail started banging against anything within two feet of her rear end. They had to get out of the house quickly and quietly. If that was possible. Bear gripped the end of her tail as they slipped out of the room, down the stairs, and out the front door.

As they walked down Wharf Street the only sound was the jangling of Honey's tags on her collar. There was no wind and the birds were still sleeping. They walked down the middle of the road to avoid the shadowy edges. The eerie quiet was broken when an owl called out. Bear gasped. Honey froze. Then Bear remembered they had to catch Hiram before he went out on his boat.

"We gotta hurry," Bear said, and they both began to run.

The bed and breakfast was completely dark when they went past, and so was the fish house. Bear didn't see any activity at the Lobstermen's Pier.

"I bet he'll go in the shack first," Bear said to Honey. "We won't miss him this way." They both sat down in front of the door that faced the water and waited.

Honey put her head in his lap. Bear could hear the soft lapping of the ocean on the sandy beach, and then a seagull squawked. The darkness slowly lifted. Maybe they had missed Hiram and the other lobstermen. Maybe they were already on their boats pulling traps. Bear closed his eyes and leaned back against the door. If he couldn't talk to Hiram, what would he do?

Then the smell came to him. Hiram was nearby. The scent of pipe smoke was faint but unmistakable. Bear and Honey jumped up and dashed around the fish house.

"Yoooow!" Hiram shouted, stepped back, and clutched his chest.

Bear and Honey jumped back at the sound of Hiram's scream.

"You scared the bejesus out of me, boy." Hiram began to chuckle. "Can't remember when I've been so shocked."

"Sorry." Bear noticed Hiram was still clutching his chest. "You okay?"

"Nearly gave me a heart attack." He smiled as he spoke. "What are you two doing up before the crack of dawn? Your grandmother throw you both out on the street?"

"No. We just need your help and some information."

"This about that lobster claw she found?" Hiram gestured to Honey.

Bear nodded. It felt like a month had passed since Hiram had taken the claw from him and tossed it into the beach grass. Hiram had warned them not threatened them. Bear understood that now.

"Those buoys, round Porcupine Island. They aren't legal. Aren't registered with the state. I did a little detective work yesterday."

"We did too. We snuck into…" Bear stopped talking and looked around.

Hiram must have understood. "Let's go out on the pier. Keep her close." As they walked, he whispered, "Sound carries over the water. Best keep our voices low."

Bear nodded his understanding and shortened Honey's leash. He didn't want her digging anything up this morning.

On the pier, he whispered and gestured in case Hiram couldn't hear him. "Underneath us is a lobster graveyard. There are shells in there that are too big, too small, have V cuts."

Hiram paused, raised his eyebrows, and looked at Bear before picking up his pace.

Bear hurried to catch up. Beside the ladder, Bear whispered and pointed. "Whose lobster car is that?"

Hiram shook his head before scrambling down the ladder, while Honey and Bear watched from above. In one motion, Hiram was on the float and opening the crate. He pulled out three lobsters. Shook his head and then put them back. He climbed back up, clearly thinking. "Get down. It'll be harder to see us." Bear sat cross-legged on the pier. Hiram squatted in front of him and whispered, "The other guys will be here soon. Tell me everything. We'll sort this out."

Bear began at the beginning, when Honey had first appeared with the monster lobster claw and then led them to the lobster graveyard. Honey seemed to nod her head in agreement.

"That's why you've been asking me all those questions."

Bear concluded by describing what they'd found in the Seabreeze kitchen the day before. "Alberta Goodhue must be cooking lobsters that are illegal."

"She's picking them and selling the meat on Sundays. That's the only way you can make money from illegal lobsters. You have to get the meat out of the shell."

"Who's catching the lobsters? She can't be doing this alone. Maybe her son Wayne, or Frank Peabody, or one of the other lobstermen."

Hiram stroked his beard. "Don't like to think it's one of the island lobstermen." He paused and looked toward Porcupine Island. "Gotta have something to do with those unregistered buoys." He rubbed the mangled fingers on his right hand. "Can't imagine Alberta pulling traps. Agree with you on that." He removed the pipe from his mouth and pointed it toward the float below them. "That lobster car. All three of those lobsters I pulled out were illegal." He tugged on his beard before speaking. "Only the boys keep live lobsters on the island and that's at the Yacht Club. Rest of us take our catch to the co-op in town. Sell it when it's fresh." Hiram stood up. "Don't tell anyone about this. I'll see you at Olivia's race. We'll make our plan after she runs."

Bear felt the vibration in the wood beneath him before he heard the footsteps of the three lobstermen walking down the pier. Bear popped to his feet as Hiram addressed the younger men. "Corker of a day. Best hurry if we're watching Olivia run." They all nodded their agreement before heading silently to their lobster boats.

The sun peeked above the horizon, casting a soft glow on the water. Everyone from Oxbow Island really was going to Olivia and Ubah's cross-country meet. Bear felt anxious for his friend. What if she decided not to run or was overwhelmed by so many people expecting so much from her? Honey sat, her eyes following Bear as he walked back and forth on the pier until the sun sat on the horizon and the lobstermen were out of sight.

"Time to go home?"

Honey jumped up in response.

"Hiram said not to tell anyone, but it's all I can think about," Bear whispered to Honey as they headed back to his grandmother's house.

"Morning, Bear," Alberta Goodhue hollered from the steps of the bed and breakfast.

Bear looked up and lifted his hand in acknowledgment. She held a broom but no buckets, and another tiny apron was tied around her generous waist. Bear picked up his pace. He would have to lock himself in his room until it was time to go to the cross-country meet if he was going to keep his mouth shut.

They burst through the front door and surprised his grandmother.

She looked at them. She looked up the stairs. "I thought you were sleeping?" It sounded like a question. She wiped her hands on a dish towel. "Where have you been?" She looked at her watch. "It's not even seven." She appeared more confused than concerned. "I really thought you were in bed." She sat down at the kitchen table without taking her eyes off of Bear and Honey. "What are you two up to now?"

Hiram's words echoed in Bear's head: *Don't tell anyone.* But his grandmother wasn't *anyone.* "Gramma," he began slowly. "Olivia and I discovered something…bad."

She didn't interrupt. She nodded her head and waited for him to say more.

"Remember how everyone said I should ask Hiram for help?"

"For your schoolwork. Is this about your research project?"

"Yes!" Bear said, quickly thinking that could end their discussion. "No. Not really." He could see her trust slipping away. "Hiram is helping us, but I promised him I wouldn't tell anybody about this until after Olivia's meet. Is that okay?"

She examined his face. "You're not in trouble?"

He shook his head and Honey offered her a paw.

"You'll explain everything tonight?"

Bear nodded and Honey laid her head on Sally Parker's lap.

"Okay." She stood up. "What do you want for breakfast?"

The rest of the day crawled. Bear and his grandmother were ready to walk to the ferry thirty minutes early. She seemed as nervous as Bear felt. The blue-and-white knit hats were in a big bag between them on the couch. His grandmother had bought dozens of them. "We could remove all the tags and fold them. I bought extra to hand out…" her voice trailed off.

Bear jumped at the opportunity to do something, anything. He ran to get the scissors.

His grandmother remained seated, picking at her fingernails. "I hope this isn't too much."

Bear plopped down next to the bag full of hats. "No. This is great. Everyone's going to want to wear one. All the lobstermen will be there—" He stopped himself.

"Really? Well, that's good. What I meant is, too much for Olivia and Ubah. I hope we haven't put too much pressure on them."

Bear nodded his head. He understood.

The ferry to Portland was loaded with excited islanders joking and talking about what a wonderful runner Olivia was and how she was going to show everyone what an island kid could do. In the middle of the pre-race celebration of anticipated victory was a quiet cluster. Bear and his grandmother sat with the Professor, Mrs. Frost, and Victor Anaya. They were a puddle of anxious, strained silence surrounded by proud neighbors. Bear thought about what his grandmother had said. What if this, the crowd of eager islanders, was too much? Olivia loved running through the woods alone. Bear chewed on a fingernail.

Victor rarely left the island. He hadn't been to any of Olivia's other cross-country meets. It was too hard for him to get from the ferry terminal to wherever a meet was being held. The Professor had arranged for a friend with an accessible van to pick them all up. While the somber group waited for the van to arrive, Bear jogged toward Commercial Street. He had to see if the guy who sold lobsters on the street was there.

Bear pressed himself against the far edge of the parking garage and stuck his head around the corner. He saw the guy less than ten feet away, talking to a customer. Bear pulled his head back around the corner and leaned against the brick building. He needed to see more of the man to identify him. Bear peeked around the corner again, just as the lobster vendor turned toward his cooler. He was wearing a big gold watch like Wayne Goodhue's, but he was thinner than Alberta's son. On his little finger, a gold ring with a large diamond flashed in the sunshine. Bear would have noticed if Wayne wore a ring like that.

Bear was preparing to sneak one more peek when a horn honked behind him. The lobster seller turned toward the sound. Bear jerked back behind the brick wall of the garage. There was something familiar about that man. Where had Bear seen him?

"Bear! Hurry! The van's here," his grandmother yelled, waving her arms. He raced to the van.

As they pulled away from the ferry terminal and turned onto Commercial Street, Bear twisted in his seat to look at the man one more time. Where had he seen him?

"That's Alberta Goodhue's *gentleman friend!*" Bear blurted into the silence of the van before clamping a hand over his mouth.

"What?" Mrs. Frost sat next to him. The others were too lost in their thoughts to even respond to Bear's comment.

"Nothing," Bear mumbled before making a motion to indicate that his lips were sealed.

Mrs. Frost looked intrigued but only nodded her head. She knew how to keep a secret.

The rest of the drive was filled with anxious silence. Everyone's hopes lay on Olivia. Bear's concerns pushed all thoughts of lobsters from his mind. Victor had left the island to see her run. The Professor had a friend get a van and drive them to the meet. The elderly and frail Mrs. Frost was going to stand in a field for at least an hour. And everyone else from the island would be there too. Olivia would run. She had to. Didn't she? And what about Ubah? Who would be there to support her? Would she be allowed to run with her hijab?

Bear slunk into the seat and exhaled loudly. Mrs. Frost patted his knee gently, but she looked as nervous as he felt.

18

Bear and his grandmother helped Mrs. Frost make the big step down from the van. The Professor leaned on a cane instead of crutches. It was a long walk to where a crowd gathered around the starting line for the meet. The islanders leaned against the van and looked toward the other spectators.

"We have a while before Olivia runs. Maybe some of us should wait in the van," Sally Parker said.

Bear knew she meant Mrs. Frost and the Professor. But it had taken forever to get them out of the van. It made no sense to have them climb back in.

"Don't worry," the Professor said. "We have chairs."

At that moment, his friend came around the back of the van with two folding chairs in his hand.

"Bear, can you carry these?"

They began the long, slow walk. Olivia could run two miles in less time than it took them to get to the start line. When they had Mrs. Frost and the Professor settled into their chairs, Bear and his grandmother looked for the blue-and-white uniforms of Olivia's team. The runners were clustered under a large, leafless oak tree on the opposite side of the open field.

Before they could get there, Olivia and Ubah ran over to join them. Ubah was wearing a blue-and-white hijab wrapped around her hair and tucked into the back of her team jersey.

"We have the hats!" Sally Parker extended the bag before hugging Olivia.

Olivia grabbed a hat and pulled it down over her ears before mumbling, "I want to talk to Dad before I run." Her voice quivered and Bear's anxiety rose. "With everyone here, I can pretend I'm running on the island." She nodded her head as she spoke, like she was trying to convince herself. She tugged on the hat until it covered her eyebrows. "This will be my lucky charm. All the girls said they'd wear one. Not the boys. They're afraid. They think the coach will punish them or something."

"You're gonna be great," Bear said as he tapped her shoulder.

Olivia ran to hug her father, who was sitting between the Professor and Mrs. Frost. He was whispering to her when they were interrupted by a man dramatically clearing his throat. Everyone turned to face the stranger in a track suit. A whistle hung around his neck.

"More island refugees." He sneered the words. "Olivia, you missed practice on Monday without a doctor's note. You're not running. Get that uniform cleaned and returned to me by eight o'clock on Monday."

Ubah slid behind Sally Parker. Bear glanced around nervously and saw Ubah's father and several other men hurrying across the open field toward them.

With the flick of a switch, Victor's wheelchair thrust forward into the coach's leg. Victor's voice boomed. "What the—"

The Professor interrupted. "Excuse me, I'm her doctor." Using his cane for balance, he struggled to move between Victor and Olivia's coach. "I wrote a note." He wobbled a bit as he towered over the coach. "I'm Dr. Malcolm Yeats, and I am confident that if you were a better organized individual you would have my note."

The coach looked uncertain before turning his attention to Ubah, who was shrinking behind Sally Parker. "What did I tell you about that head scarf?" His arm reached over Sally Parker's shoulder in an attempt to grab it. The hook of Mrs. Frost's wooden cane encircled his wrist and pulled his hand away.

In that moment, the girls' cross-country team enveloped Ubah and Olivia and ushered them to the start line for the girls' race. Ubah's father, friends, and the residents of Oxbow Island formed a human wall between the coach and the girls' team.

As the coach stormed off, a skinny boy with a headful of red curls approached Sally Parker. Behind him, the rest of the boys' cross-country team stood silently, watching. "Excuse me. I'm Ezrah. Do you have any more of those hats?" He pointed at the one on Victor's head.

Sally Parker's hand shook as she handed the bag to Ezrah. "Thank you." Her head nodded. "Thank you."

Bear turned to the Professor. "You're not a doctor."

"I beg your pardon. I have a doctorate in English literature and my students all address me as *Doctor*."

Bear laughed. "But you didn't write Olivia a note."

"Actually, I did."

Bear's jaw dropped.

"Not about her health. Obviously. And it was for her English teacher, not the coach. But these are all minor details."

Mr. Daahir interrupted. "Hurry. Hurry. They are about to start. We saved a spot at the front for you." He gestured toward the Professor and Mrs. Frost. Victor was already racing to an opening in the assembled crowd.

Bear was so nervous; his feet were frozen in place. He chewed on his thumbnail. He didn't want to see Olivia and Ubah lose. A hand gently touched Bear's shoulder. He looked up into the eyes of Mr. Daahir.

Ubah's father leaned toward him and spoke with quiet confidence. "Unity is power. Our girls will be strong today." He nodded once. "Come." Together they hurried to join the crowd lining the start of the racecourse.

The starting gun exploded, and the huddled group watched nine girls with blue-and-white hats and one with a blue-and-white scarf burst from the starting line. They surged in front of the others in a tight, protective pack. When Olivia had said they all stuck together, Bear had imagined a slow-moving blob. But those girls looked as powerful as a freight train. Within seconds, Olivia and Ubah emerged at the front of the team, running side by side. Two by two, the rest of the team fell in close behind, flying across the meadow toward the trail that ran through the woods.

When all of the blue-and-white uniforms had disappeared into the woods, the assembled group became silent. They had no way of knowing what was happening on the trails hidden from view. Maybe their girls had gone out too fast and used up precious energy. Someone could trip and fall. Another team might have a better strategy and be reserving their energy for a strong finish. There was no way to know. The spectators were frozen in place, staring at the opening in the woods where the runners would emerge onto the field.

Twelve minutes later, Victor threw his arms up into the air and let out a loud "Whoop!" Had he recognized Olivia through the trees or sensed her presence?

It was a moment before anyone else spotted her exiting the woods. She was alone. Bear had seen her run many times, but never like this. He was sure her feet weren't touching the ground. She was flying, not running. Her head was high, her eyes focused on her island family clustered at the finish line. Victor sat between the Professor and Mrs. Frost with everyone screaming behind them. The three gripped each other's hands, silently watching as Olivia charged toward them.

More shouting erupted next to them. It was Ubah's friends and family. Bear looked back toward the opening in the woods. Ubah emerged, racing, striding onto the field, her blue-and-white scarf streaming behind her as her family and friends hopped up and down. The women's long, graceful garments amplified their excitement as they gripped each other's hands with joy. Olivia and Ubah were the only girls crossing the field. Bear scanned the crowd. Everyone was cheering. Everyone was screaming for Olivia and Ubah. He tapped his grandmother and pointed. She nodded as tears streamed down her face at the sight.

Olivia crossed the finish line and jumped over the ropes to hug her father.

Other girls came out of the woods now, too far back to catch Ubah. Two more girls were dressed in the blue-and-white uniform of Olivia and Ubah's team.

Ubah crossed the finish line, came to a complete stop, and shrieked with joy before clamping her hands over her mouth. She managed to step out of the chute before falling to her knees and crying. She was immediately surrounded by the women in her family and concealed by a protective cloud of flowing fabric.

"Maybe Ubah isn't as quiet as we thought," Bear said to his grandmother.

"She found her voice."

More girls crossed the finish line. Three more of Olivia and Ubah's teammates were in the top twenty finishers.

"I think we won," Olivia said. "We must have. There's no way we didn't. We're going to the State Championships!" Olivia shook her head in surprise before running to congratulate her teammates.

Bear looked around him. Ubah's family and friends talked and laughed with the Oxbow Island lobstermen and Olivia's friends and neighbors. Many wore the extra blue-and-white knit hats his grandmother had bought. Members of the boys' team congratulated the girls. On the far side of the field, Olivia's coach stood alone beneath the barren oak tree. His team had beaten everyone's expectations, but he wasn't celebrating.

Hiram Wiley commanded everyone's attention when he said to Olivia, "I always knew you'd make us proud." He patted her on the back. "The boys and I"—he gestured toward the lobstermen standing behind him—"have planned a special parade for our island champion."

Olivia's face broke into a huge smile, but Bear was confused. "Parade? What did he mean, *parade*?"

"A lobster boat parade!" Olivia shrieked.

Bear didn't fully understand until the meet was over and every Oxbow Island resident was loaded onto a boat. All of the lobster boats flew blue-and-white flags at their sterns. There was also a scallop dragger, a tugboat, and a small barge. They pulled out of the harbor and fell into line, idling in place until the red-and-black fireboat steamed to the front of the line with its blue lights flashing. Bear and Olivia whooped at the sight. The boat leading their celebration was usually associated with sickness, injury, disaster, and even death. When the fireboat began spraying water high into the air from four different nozzles, they were stunned into silence.

Olivia stood with her hands over her mouth.

"That's for you," Bear said.

She shook her head.

"Is running fun again?" he asked.

Hiram stood by their side. "Never get tired of that sight."

They were the only people on Hiram's boat, so they could speak openly. "Hey, Hi," Bear said. "I saw the guy who sells lobsters in Portland. It's Alberta Goodhue's *gentleman friend*."

"I know who he is, and he's no gentleman," Hiram began. "That's Pinky Browne. He's from up by the border. Been working his way down the coast ever since he lost his lobster license. Marine Patrol has been trying to catch him for years. Looks like you two found him."

Olivia and Bear bumped fists and shouted "Kaboom!"

"But—" Hiram gave them a serious look. "This could get dangerous. It's time for law enforcement to step in."

"But—"

"We can help—"

"Really—"

Hiram put up a hand to stop Bear and Olivia. "You'll help. We need you to keep Alberta Goodhue in the B and B. Keep her from leaving or looking out the front windows from eight to nine tomorrow morning. She can see the whole harbor from there, and we don't want her to warn Pinky. You think you can do that?"

"Yes!" they answered together without hesitating.

Later that night, as they were finishing the pumpkin pyramid, they tried to figure out how they were going to distract Alberta Goodhue. She always seemed to be on the front steps when they went by. They knew they couldn't just tie her to a chair and lock the door, although they liked the idea.

The grown-ups were visiting by candlelight on Mrs. Frost's front porch. Zoe had parked the taxi in Sally Parker's front yard with the headlights aimed at the pumpkin pyramid so they could see what they were doing. She played her guitar and sang as Bear and Olivia considered the possibilities: show up with a board game or puzzle, ask to see all the guest rooms, ask to borrow something, invite her to coffee at Bear's grandmother's…

"When are we going to make our costumes if we have to distract that woman?" Bear wondered out loud.

"If we tie her up then we can come back here and make them," Olivia joked.

19

When Bear and Honey came downstairs for breakfast on Halloween morning, Olivia sat at the kitchen table. His grandmother sat at the opposite end, warming her hands on her coffee mug. Motionless and silent, they appeared to be in some sort of standoff. Bear and Honey stopped and waited; not sure it was wise to take another step.

"Good morning, Buckaroo Bear," his grandmother grinned, breaking the silence and moving to the stove. "I believe you promised to tell me about a secret you and Hiram have." She started mixing the batter for pancakes. "I can't get a word out of Olivia. But I suspect she's here for more than just the pancakes."

Olivia grinned. "Maybe."

Bear explained: they had found illegal lobsters shells, and Alberta Goodhue was involved. "The lobster meat she sells on Sundays is from lobsters that are too big, too little, or egg-bearing. She's getting them from a guy named Pinky Browne."

"Some kind of lobster fugitive," Olivia added.

"They're arresting them this morning. We have to make sure Alberta doesn't leave the B and B."

"How do you do that? Hold her hostage? I don't like the sound of this." Bear's grandmother flipped a pancake and it missed the pan. She groaned.

"No, no," Bear said. "I thought we could just talk to her. Distract her."

"She could be like a wild animal, cornered," Sally Parker said as she dropped the ruined pancake into Honey's food dish. "Have you ever noticed, she's always in front of the B and B or comes out when you walk by? It's like she's watching for something. Someone."

Bear laughed at his grandmother. "She looks like Mrs. Claus. How dangerous can she be?"

"Looks can be deceiving." She placed the syrup and butter on the table. "And what about your Halloween costumes? You haven't made them, have you? I'll distract her and you two stay here and make your costumes."

"No!" Olivia and Bear shouted before looking at each other.

"I was wondering if you could make our costumes," Bear said. "Catching these guys is really important. Hiram needs us."

Sally Parker stood with her hands on her hips, looking back and forth between Olivia and Bear. "I can't let you go down there alone."

"You'll blow our cover!"

"No. I'll just be walking Honey."

"But she started all this." Bear pointed at Honey, who was sleeping soundly on the kitchen floor. "And what about our costumes?" Bear begged. When he saw the look in his grandmother's eyes, he knew it was a lost cause. She was coming with them. "You cannot let her off leash. Or let her go anywhere on that beach." He sounded like his grandmother. Bear looked at Olivia. "What about our costumes?"

"Mrs. Frost will be happy to help. What do you want to be?" his grandmother asked.

Bear popped up from the table, jumped over Honey, and raced upstairs to his bedroom. He found the two giant lobster claws in his closet under the dirty laundry.

His grandmother's eyes widened at the sight of the claws.

"I'm a lobster monster and Olivia's a giant lobster trap."

"I thought we couldn't show those to anyone," Olivia said. "You can't take them trick-or-treating."

"Hiram said it's okay. By tonight everyone will know who caught them."

"We better get a move on," his grandmother said as she took the claws from him. "You two head down. I'll run these over to Viola and explain your costumes. I'll be a few minutes behind you so nobody suspects. Scream if anything goes wrong. Promise?"

They both nodded and rose from the kitchen table.

They moved slowly down Wharf Street. Olivia and Bear each kicked a pebble ahead of them as they walked.

"We still don't have a plan." Bear scanned the harbor. "Who's in that dinghy?" He pointed toward the Lobstermen's Pier. "Are we too late?"

"It could be anyone," Olivia said. "We should hurry." She stopped walking and looked at Bear. "Fall down and hurt yourself."

"You fall down and hurt yourself," Bear replied.

"That wouldn't be believable." Olivia dismissed his comment. "You need to bleed. Then we burst into the B and B. She'll want to bandage you up."

Bear agreed with that. "Then what? That won't take more than ten minutes."

"We'll figure something out," Olivia said. "Do you want me to push you?"

"No!" Bear stepped away from her. "Don't!"

Olivia raised her hands as if to give him a shove. Bear turned and ran down the hill, ten steps, fifteen steps. Slide into home base, he told himself. And took five more steps. He could see the back of the bed and breakfast. He was running out of road. Now! He threw himself into a belly flop. He had hoped the palms of his hands would be scraped and bloody, but when Olivia caught up with him, her shocked expression told him the damage was more impressive. He rolled onto his back and they both grimaced.

"Are you okay? I didn't mean *hurt* hurt yourself."

Now he felt it. His chin must have bounced off the road. The old wound opened up. It was throbbing. His hands stung, and he'd ripped his pants on the knees. They were bleeding too. There was dirt and grit imbedded in every wound. He hurt all over but sat up and glanced toward the harbor. "We gotta go. That dinghy is leaving the float."

"We have to get inside. It won't work if she patches you up out here."

"And keep her away from the harborside windows."

Olivia ran into the Seabreeze Bed and Breakfast, hollering, "Alberta, help!" with Bear hobbling behind her.

Alberta burst out of the kitchen and pulled the door shut behind her as Frank Peabody rushed down the stairs.

"Stop hollering. You'll wake the guests." He was mad. Then he saw Bear. "Oh, no. What happened? Sit." He pulled a fancy upholstered chair toward Bear in spite of the dirt and blood that covered him. "Alberta, get the first aid kit from the bathroom."

As she bustled down the hall, Bear and Olivia looked at each other. As soon as she disappeared into the bathroom, they raced behind her, slammed the door shut, and sat on the floor pressing their backs against the door. Within seconds she was pounding on the door.

"What are you two doing?" Frank Peabody strode toward them. His face was red, and his lips were pulled into a tight circle. "Explain yourselves. Now!"

Bear and Olivia spoke over each other trying to explain.

"Please. You have to trust us."

"Check the kitchen."

"Look for white buckets."

"She's got illegal lobsters."

Alberta Goodhue began to scream. It was a shrill, ugly sound. This was nothing like her sweet, lilting voice. This wasn't even human. They all covered their ears. Frank headed to the kitchen. Bear hoped she had lobsters in there. If she didn't, Frank would never believe them. What would they do then?

The door began to slam against their backs and Olivia and Bear dug in their heels, but it was hard to keep from sliding on the tile floor. She must be throwing her whole body against the door. A gorilla would be impressed by her strength. If she kept this up, Bear's back would be as battered as his front.

Sally Parker burst through the front door. "I heard screams." She stopped abruptly and barely avoided colliding with three guests in their pajamas who had rushed down the stairs. She pushed through the pajama-clad guests and dropped to the floor beside Bear as Alberta slammed the door into their backs. They all grimaced and braced their heels against the tile floor, preparing for the next battering.

The guests in their pajamas stood at the bottom of the stairs and stared. If they had any idea how ridiculous they looked, they would not be gawking at Olivia, Bear, and his grandmother, Bear thought. One woman was in a fluffy pink bathrobe with rollers in her hair, another wore a very short and lacy red nightgown, and the man wore shiny black pajamas covered with penguins. At first, they seemed confused, but then they became concerned about the screaming woman in the bathroom. They wanted to free Alberta Goodhue.

After several moments of "Get away from the door" and "Let that poor woman out," they went into a whispering huddle. Suddenly the penguin pajama man ran down the hallway. He grabbed Olivia by the ankles and dragged her across the floor. As she was sliding, she managed to punch and kick her way out of his grasp.

Frank Peabody stepped out of the kitchen. "Stop! Don't touch that girl." His hands were full of watches, necklaces, and bracelets. "Get away from her now."

The penguin pajama man rubbed his arms and shins where Olivia had made solid contact as he rejoined the female guests at the bottom of the stairs. They turned to look at the innkeeper.

"That's my necklace," the woman in the short red nightgown said. "Why do you have my necklace?"

Alberta Goodhue stopped screaming and pounding. Still, Frank Peabody sat on the floor in Olivia's place, adding his weight to the door. "The police are coming. We'll sort everything out then," he answered before turning to Bear and Olivia. "They are coming. Aren't they?"

"Go check," Bear said to Olivia. "I hurt too much to move."

"Oh, no, Bear. Did she hurt you?" his grandmother asked.

Bear knew his grandmother was referring to Alberta Goodhue, but he couldn't resist replying, "Yes, Olivia pushed me."

"Did not." Olivia said from the window. "Wow!" She turned and looked at them. "Wow! Wow! Wow!" Everyone in pajamas joined her at the window.

"Tell us!" Bear and his grandmother said.

"Betty and Liz Bucknam are on the beach on their horses. Officer Calvin's police car is down there with the lights flashing. I'm pretty sure that's the Marine Patrol boat." The guests seemed to have forgotten about the jewelry in Frank Peabody's hands as they watched all the activity in the harbor. Olivia looked out the window again. "I think the Coast Guard boat is coming. And that dinghy, the one we saw earlier. It's flying this way!"

Bear wished he could take in the excitement, but he wasn't sure he could stand. His grandmother was trying to pick the gravel out of his bloody knees, but it just made them hurt more. "Stop. Please." He moved her hand. "Gramma, where's Honey?"

Olivia whirled around at the window. "Where's Honey? She better not be digging up the evidence."

Bear jumped up, wincing from the pain in his knees, and pushed past the pajama people at the window. He scanned the beach for the golden retriever.

There was a crashing sound as Alberta Goodhue slammed into the door, and it opened several inches. The man in the penguin pajamas sat down beside Sally Parker. He was big enough Alberta was not getting out of the bathroom.

"Oh, no. When I heard the scream, I must have dropped the leash," Sally Parker said. "I don't know. I was so scared. I thought something had gone wrong. Bear, you have to find her."

"Pinky Browne won't go to the pier with the horses there and Officer Calvin on the beach." Bear was thinking out loud as he looked down on all the activity in the harbor. Pinky was being chased toward shore by the Marine Patrol and the Coast Guard. "There's that trail that comes out at the graveyard." He pointed toward the Seafarers Museum. "Remember? We slid down it."

Olivia and Bear bolted from the bed and breakfast. Bear couldn't keep up. He shouted at Officer Calvin as he hobbled behind Olivia. He could hear Honey barking. It sounded like she was at the top of the trail. Officer Calvin and the horses and riders on the beach looked in his direction before trotting over.

"There's a trail up from the water." He pointed toward Olivia's back and the sound of Honey barking. "Comes out on the museum's lawn. To the right of the graveyard. He must be trying to escape that way." Bear looked toward the water. The dinghy and its passenger had disappeared. But the ferry was pulling into the dock beside the Coast Guard cutter and the Marine Patrol boat. The Oxbow Island Harbor had never been so busy.

Olivia was out of sight by the time Bear had finished explaining. The horses galloped toward the barking dog. Bear turned to Officer Calvin. "Alberta Goodhue's blocked in the B and B's bathroom and Frank Peabody has a bunch of jewelry."

"Well done. I'll pick her up. Go get your dog. The humans can take over now."

When Bear arrived at the trailhead, Honey was seated at the top of the cliff, staring at Pinky Browne's face. Only his head poked above the cliff, and it swiveled from the dog in front of him to Chester Frost's headstone beside him to the ocean far below.

Betty Bucknam slid off her horse and handed the reins to Bear. "Call your dog."

Honey trotted to Bear's side before he spoke, her leash trailing behind her. She was replaced by the harbor master at the top of the cliff.

"Up or down? It makes no difference to me." Betty Bucknam extended a hand to Pinky Browne. He hesitated, looked beneath him at the water and the boats in the harbor, and decided he'd rather surrender to the harbor master. She pulled him onto the lawn before removing handcuffs from her back pocket.

As they walked toward the bed and breakfast, Bear saw ferry passengers coming up from the dock. Wayne Goodhue turned onto Water Street and approached them. He shook his head at the sight of the horses and his mother's *gentleman friend* being escorted down the street. "Pinky...what—"

Pinky turned away from him.

Wayne saw the handcuffs and the gold watch. "Is that my watch?" Pinky stared at the ground. "You took my watch." Wayne shook his head and turned toward the bed and breakfast as his mother was being escorted out the front door by Officer Calvin. Behind her was a mix of familiar islanders and strangers in pajamas. But Wayne remained focused on his mother.

Bear expected Wayne to lose his temper: yell at Officer Calvin, demand to know what was going on, defend his mother. But he didn't do any of those things. He stared at her and slowly shook his head until Alberta Goodhue was standing in front of him. She still looked like Mrs. Claus in a tiny apron, but her hands were cuffed behind her back. Bear looked back and forth between the mother and son. There was no anger or confusion on Wayne Goodhue's face, only sadness. "Mom, you promised—"

She interrupted him. "I didn't do nothing. It's all him." She tipped her head toward Pinky Browne, who sat in the island police car. "Honest, Wayne. It's all a big misunderstanding. You'll see."

"I'm so disappointed, Mom." Wayne turned to walk back to the dock as the ferry was departing.

Betty Bucknam stopped him. "They'll have to hold onto your watch as evidence but they'll return it later." She had removed Wayne's watch from Pinky Browne's wrist. "We can give you a ride to town on the Marine Patrol boat with these two. It'll be an hour before the next ferry."

"No. Thanks. I'd rather wait." He walked away, his shoulders sagging.

Bear hated it when he disappointed his parents. Watching Wayne, he realized that being disappointed by your parents was even worse.

20

"Every time you visit, we have a crime wave," Officer Calvin said and reached out to shake Bear's hand. Bear held both hands up, revealing the bloody scrapes embedded with gravel on his palms. The police officer knelt and shook Honey's paw instead. "Thank you for helping us catch those two." As John Calvin stood, he noticed Bear's ripped pants and bloody knees. "You want the EMT to clean you up?"

"No, I'm good."

"Hope that's not your Halloween costume." Pointing to Bear's chin, he said, "I think you need more blood on your face if you expect to get any candy."

Bear and Olivia reacted. "Our costumes. What time is it?"

Olivia began running up Wharf Street before pausing to look back at Bear limping behind her. She smiled and waited for him. "I think you look bad enough that could be your costume."

"Thanks."

Sally Parker and Honey joined them. "Let's see what Viola has been up to." She put an arm around Bear's shoulders and gave him a side hug as they moved up the hill. "You two make me very proud."

"I'm glad you were there," Bear said. "When you came through that door—" He shook his head, remembering the moment. "I've never been so happy to see you."

"We couldn't have held her in there for another minute," Olivia added.

"Frank said she's been stealing jewelry from the guests for weeks. He never suspected her, and he didn't know about the lobsters either."

"She doesn't look like a criminal," Bear said. "She looks like…a grandmother, like Mrs. Claus."

"You can be both," Olivia said as they turned onto Maple Street.

Stopping in front of Sally Parker's house, they admired their pumpkin pyramid. It was impressive from a distance, filling half the front yard and looming over the front porch. Bear and Olivia bumped fists. "Kaboom!"

Zoe's taxi was parked in Mrs. Frost's yard, where Zoe stood, marveling at the massive pyramid with Victor and Hiram. Where were Mrs. Frost and the Professor? Bear looked toward the porch but didn't see them.

"Do you think it's the biggest in the world?" Olivia asked.

"Does that matter?" Sally Parker said. "I think it's amazing!"

Bear and Olivia grinned.

Hiram joined them. "Thank you." He shook Olivia's hand then turned to Bear but pulled his hand back when he saw the palms of Bear's hands. "I'm impressed."

Bear blushed and his chest swelled with pride. Those words from Hiram Wiley were better than any certificate from the governor. Bear and Olivia ducked their heads and remained frozen in place.

"Don't we have some costumes to check on?" Sally Parker said as she squeezed their shoulders. "You two do manage to pack a lot into a week. That's for sure."

Hiram chuckled and walked with them. "Olivia, hope you don't mind, I volunteered to help Viola with your costume. Time was short and we improvised."

Olivia ran up Mrs. Frost's porch steps as Bear hobbled behind her, eager to see what their neighbor had created. They burst through the front door and found Mrs. Frost and the Professor hard at work. Two sewing machines were pushed to the back of the puzzle table as Mrs. Frost duct-taped two long pieces of bubble wrap together.

"We're not finished, Berend," Mrs. Frost said. "You can try it on in a minute." She looked up for the first time and saw Bear's scratches and scrapes. "Oh, no. Not again. What happened? Who hurt you?"

"Olivia." He stepped aside before she could punch him in the shoulder.

"I did not. He…never mind."

Bear looked at all the clear plastic surrounding them and the rolls of silver duct tape and wondered how that could become a lobster. How could he ask? No lobster ever started out looking like that. "Mrs. Frost—"

"Don't worry about a thing. You're not my first lobster."

Zoe burst through the door with two cans of spray paint. "I found more." She saw Bear's confused face and added, "I use it on the taxi. It says 'cherry red,' but it could be called 'boiled-lobster red.'"

"Try this on." Mrs. Frost handed him a giant tube made of bubble wrap. "We'll spray paint it once we know it fits." Bear wiggled into his lobster body. "The tail will flow behind you, but the Professor will add a string so you can move it up and down."

"We'll attach the real claws here," the Professor said as he pointed to a hidden snap and tab.

When all the pieces were in place, Bear turned so everyone could see him.

"You need antennae," Hiram said. "Otherwise, I'd say you're a keeper."

"Ni-ice." Olivia made it sound like two syllables.

"Olivia, can you run up to the attic and see if you can find a red swim cap, two metal hangers, and there should be more bubble wrap? I'd ask Berend, but he's a bit banged up."

Olivia hesitated.

"It's pretty organized," Bear reassured her. "Packing supplies are in that corner." He pointed. "I've seen metal hangers near them, and the swim cap is probably in the opposite corner with the summer stuff, next to a pile of puzzles."

"When you get out of that costume, I'll take it outside to paint," Zoe said to Bear.

Hiram walked in carrying an oversized lobster trap and some bait bags. "I thought you could use these for your candy." He held the bait bags out for Bear, who recoiled. "They're new. I just made them. The holes are small, so your candy won't fall out, but the bags are big to hold more candy."

"What's that?" Bear asked, pointing to the extra-large lobster trap with the hole in the middle and what looked like leather belts attached to the top.

"Olivia's costume," Hiram said as Olivia came down the stairs.

"It's like a warehouse up there," Olivia said as she handed the materials to Mrs. Frost.

"Waste not, want not," Mrs. Frost said.

"Want to try this on?" Hiram asked Olivia. He picked up the metal costume. "Hope it's not too heavy." He unhooked two latches on one side and the circle opened up, thanks to hinges on the opposite side. Hiram placed the suspenders on Olivia's shoulders before closing the hollow center around her waist and hips. "Is that comfortable? We can move it up or down with the suspenders."

Olivia stepped away from him and said, "What do you think?" She grinned. "I'm a lobster trap!"

"Hiram made bait bags for our candy." Bear was excited, but Olivia's face looked as disgusted as his had when he first heard.

Before Bear could explain, Sally Parker came in. "Let's get some food into you," she said to Olivia and Bear. "Can you finish the costumes without these two?" she asked the grown-ups.

Olivia and Bear collapsed at Sally Parker's kitchen table. Bear's grandmother bustled around, alternating between making grilled-cheese sandwiches and cleaning the gravel out of Bear's scrapes. He settled into his chair, exhausted. Thinking through the morning's adventures, he felt a mixture of emotions flow through him: excitement and pride and gratitude for his island friends and neighbors. At this moment they were making a Halloween costume for him while he waited for lunch to be served.

"Do you think when they spray-paint it, it will look more like a lobster?" he asked Olivia. As grateful as he was, he still had doubts.

"Yup." He must not have looked convinced. She continued, "Right now I can see you through the bubble wrap. It looks like you were swallowed by a see-through fish." She paused. "Actually, that would be a really cool costume!" A grilled-cheese sandwich appeared in front of her. "Thanks," she said to Bear's grandmother, then turned back to Bear. "When Zoe paints it, then you'll be a lobster." She picked up a sandwich half. "Mrs. Frost's attic has more stuff than Marden's Surplus."

Bear and his grandmother laughed.

"Comes in handy," Sally Parker said as she placed Bear's sandwich in front of him before mussing his hair affectionately. "You two eat up. You won't have dinner until late."

After lunch, Bear looked at the kitchen clock. They had four hours left until they were allowed at Mrs. Frost's house and could see their costumes. He kicked the table leg repeatedly.

"Stop it," his grandmother and Olivia said.

"What are we supposed to do?" He started kicking the table again.

His grandmother put a hand on his shoulder. "Your schoolwork? What about your schoolwork?"

Bear groaned and slumped in his chair.

"We can graph your data," Olivia said.

"I already have a chart." Bear wanted to focus on Halloween not ocean density and salinity.

"Perfect. We can use that to make a graph. Maybe more than one graph. Who knows?" Bear started kicking the table leg again. "Graphs make it easier to see trends. They're like an illustration of your data. At least that's what my teacher said."

With both his grandmother and Olivia smiling at him, Bear rose and went upstairs to his bedroom for his notebook. When he returned to the kitchen, his grandmother had cleared the table and replaced their lunch dishes with markers, rulers and wrapping paper.

"Wrapping paper?" Bear asked.

"We can use the back for the graphs," Olivia explained.

Bear hadn't thought of that. There wasn't a store on the island that sold posterboard or any other school supplies. "Good idea."

When the graphs were finished and they had put everything away, only five minutes remained. Olivia and Bear sat in silence. They stared at the clock, urging time to move faster until the minute hand pointed straight up. Without putting on their coats and mittens, they raced next door.

Mrs. Frost and the Professor hadn't moved in hours, but they were working with different materials when Olivia and Bear barged through the front door. They were too excited to see anything other than their costumes. They swooped up the painted bubble wrap and metal cage.

"The spray paint makes all the difference. Do you think my tail will stay on?" Bear asked as he twisted to look back. His tail reached five feet behind him. There were four separate bulging sections leading to a flat, curving piece that resembled a flipper. "My antennae?"

Mrs. Frost gestured for him to approach, but when she tried to put the cap on his head it was clear that the ends of the metal hangers were going to dig into his scalp. "Head up to the attic and see if you can find something to cushion that."

Olivia and Bear waddled to the bottom of the steps before they realized there was no way they could walk up two flights of stairs wearing their bulky costumes. They quickly removed them and hurried to Mrs. Frost's attic storage. After a thorough search of the tightly packed and dimly lit space, they returned to the living room with handfuls of soft, cushioning quilt batting.

They stopped abruptly when they saw the Professor and Mrs. Frost standing in front of them. The tall Professor was made even taller by his lobster buoy costume. He wore a beanie on his head with a dowel sticking into the air above him like an antenna. Nearly eight feet in the air, ropes dangled from the top of his buoy stick. He had to tilt his head so the stick didn't hit the ceiling. His arms jutted awkwardly out to the sides, and beneath the buoy was what must be the woman's half-slip gripping his knees together, barely resembling a lumpy, bumpy underwater buoy stick. Bear and Olivia collapsed into each other, laughing hysterically. And then they noticed tiny Mrs. Frost with an exceptionally dignified expression on her face and her hands clasped calmly in front of her. But what was she wearing? She was standing in a giant crocheted rope bag with drawstrings around her neck. Her arms and ankles stuck through four holes that were a little larger than the rest.

"I'm a bait bag," she said proudly.

Before they could respond, there was a knock on the door. They opened it to find Bear's grandmother, who shouted, "Trick or treat!" She spun around so they could see her costume. "I don't think I'll fit through the door. I got dressed on our front porch and almost fell when I walked down the front steps."

Bear stared at his grandmother. Her head protruded from a forest-green mound of felt. Around the bottom of the felt was an irregular strip in different shades of gray, and below that was a mix of blue, green, and white. "Are those waves?" Bear pointed to the strip of fabric that circled his grandmother several feet from the ground." "Did that start out as an umbrella?"

Olivia joined Bear at the door, tilted her head, and asked, "Are you Porcupine Island?"

"I am!" Sally Parker hopped with pleasure and the fabric waves crashed around her knees. "Viola made it. It's a work of art. Look at the details in the rocks." She held up the fabric for them to see before noticing they weren't in their costumes. "Bear, Olivia, hurry up and get dressed. Everyone's waiting for you."

When they stepped onto the front porch, there was a small gathering. Victor was the first to greet them. "You're a lobster too!" Bear said.

"Yes, and I'm motorized!" Victor's lobster costume was horizontal with the claws sticking out in front of the wheelchair's armrests and the giant tail floating behind him. His arms and hands were hidden inside the costume.

"Can your tail go up and down?" Bear raised and lowered his right wrist, and his tail responded by bouncing on the porch. "Good thing Alberta Goodhue's gone, or she'd be boiling us up right now," Bear joked. "I still can't believe she's a criminal. She looks just like Mrs. Claus. Right?"

"Exactly." Victor lifted his giant lobster claws toward Bear's face and said, "Mrs. Claws!"

Bear didn't laugh as hard as Victor did, but he had to admit that was pretty funny.

"Be careful. There's a lobster boat over there," Victor said as the taxi horn honked.

Bear looked toward the road. Somehow Zoe had turned the taxi into a cherry-red lobster boat. Bear and Olivia raced to see how she had made it.

"You can make just about anything with cardboard and duct tape," she said as she slipped out the back door. All the other doors were blocked by a perfectly formed cardboard hull covered with a shiny coat of cherry-red spray paint. "Of course, there's no deck but you can use your imagination. I'm going to drive around and throw candy out the windows. Want some?"

Olivia eagerly placed some in her bait bag, but Bear's hands were trapped inside his lobster claws. Olivia put a few pieces in the bait bag strapped to Bear's wrist.

"Can we go trick-or-treating now?" Bear asked his grandmother.

"Look at your pumpkin pyramid."

"Wow!" Someone had carved the top pumpkin and placed a lit candle in it.

"That's beautiful," Olivia said. "Who? How?"

"Who's that?" Bear pointed down Maple Street toward a figure that was struggling to walk. From a distance it looked like a gigantic hot dog was approaching. As the person got closer it was clear that whatever was between the buns was a little too pink and a little too lumpy to be a hot dog. "It's a

lobster roll," Bear yelled, moving as fast as his bruised lobster legs could go to see who was inside the costume. "Mr. Mooney! But you said—"

"Trick or treat!" The store owner chuckled.

Acknowledgments

I'm indebted to my island community for their support, encouragement and inspiration. This book would not exist without the characters that surround me every day. My first readers: Mary Anderson, Marty Braun, Ruth Butler, Deqa Dhalac, Stephanie Fullam, Eileen Lee, Judy and Chip Nelson brought diverse experiences and perspectives to my manuscript. Kindly identifying confusion and wrongheadedness is a skill they all have in abundance. Jane Eklund's edits and insights improved and sharpened my plot. Jamie Hogan contributed more than illustrations to this book; our conversations helped to shape *The Lobster Graveyard*. She has been a valued sounding board and cheerleader since the inception of the *Oxbow Island Gang* series. Thank you all for helping me polish my ideas and turn them into a story fit to be shared with the world.